PROSE
BOWL

Novels by Bill Pronzini and Barry N. Malzberg

Prose Bowl
Night Screams
Acts of Mercy
The Running of Beasts

Anthologies Edited by Bill Pronzini and Barry N. Malzberg

Those We Call Monsters
Shared Tomorrows: Science Fiction in Collaboration
The End of Summer: Science Fiction of the Fifties
Dark Sins, Dark Dreams: Crime in Science Fiction

PROSE
BOWL

BILL PRONZINI and
BARRY N. MALZBERG

St. Martin's Press
New York

First Edition

Library of Congress Cataloging in Publication Data

Pronzini, Bill.
  Prose Bowl.

  I. Malzberg, Barry N., joint author. II. Title.
PZ4.P9653Pr   [PS3566.R67]   813'.54   80-14208
ISBN 0-312-65194-5

This one is for

Arthur K. Barnes	C.M. Kornbluth
Leigh Brackett	Henry Kuttner
Fredric Brown	Ed Earl Repp
Cleve Cartmill	Nat Schachner
Ray Cummings	Stanley Weinbaum
Edmond Hamilton	Robert Moore Williams
Malcolm Jameson	Arthur Leo Zagat

—Requiescant in pace

Writing is like prostitution . . . first you do it for the love of it, then you do it for a few friends, and finally you do it for money.

—Molière

Try Benzedrine inhalant first before you get yourself into all [the] lousy complications that have to do with the purveying of prose in America. Maybe it will satisfy you so well you'll decide that writing can't hold a candle to it and you'll give up all thought of writing. Not that you could, nor that I could, in any way influence you, nor any editor in any way harm you, *if* you are *really a writer.* And if you are not really a writer, but must write or die, why don't you go die? What is there so horrible about dying? Millions of people do it every day without any serious after-effects.

—Jack Woodford
How to Write for Money

Mud, mud, glorious mud,
Nothing quite like it for cooling the blood;
So follow me, follow—
Down to the hollow—
And there we shall wallow in mud
Glo-o-o-o-ri-ous mud!

—"The Song of the Hippopotamus"
Flanders and Swann
At the Drop of a Hat: Musical Revue, 1962

PROSE
BOWL

PART ONE

The Metaphor Kid

1

THE BLACKJACK KID SNARLED, "HERE'S LEAD IN YOUR GUTS, LAWMAN!" AND FILLED HIS HAND WITH TWO POUNDS OF COLT PEACEMAKER. BUT THE MARSHAL SLAPPED LEATHER WITH A GREASED-LIGHTNING SPEED OF HIS OWN. HIS HOG-LEG SPAT FLAME AN INSTANT BEFORE THE OUT-LAW'S. THE KID'S SHOT WAS WILD, BUT THE MARSHAL'S WAS STRAIGHT AND TRUE. BLACKJACK FOLDED UP LIKE A SALOON DANCER'S FAN AND TOOK HIS LAST BITE FROM THE DRY ALKALI DUST OF CIMARRON CITY'S MAIN STREET.

"Way to go, Sackett! That's how to hack it!"

I hit the carriage return key, saw that I had come to the bottom of the page, and snap-rolled it out of the typewriter. All around me the screaming of the Sackett Boosters and the rest of the seventy thousand fans seemed to ripple and flow like surf, to echo in rebounding waves off the great plastoid dome overhead. But it didn't bother me, didn't affect my concentration. And neither did being on national TriDim in front of a New-Sport audience estimated to be fifty million or so for the Prose Bowl East Coast semifinals. There was too much at stake for me to care how many people watched Rex Sackett, The Metaphor Kid, go head-to-head against the Kansas City Flash.

High on the southern rim of the Ultradome, facing me,

one of the huge electronic scoreboards blazed with numerals and prose printout. I glanced up at it as I slid a clean sheet of paper into my machine, checking the score for the first time since the start of the fourth quarter.

SACKETT 7590, GARBOWITZ 7441.

A 150-word lead now, twenty more than I'd had when the period began. And only 410 left to go in the Face-Off. Time was running out on the Flash, and he had to know it as well as I did. I gave his printout a quick scan to see how he was holding up.

ARABELLA REMEMBERED THE FIRST TIME THE DOCTOR HAD KISSED HER. OH, THE ECSTASY OF HIS LIPS ON HERS! THE THRILL OF HIS STRONG ARMS ENCIRCLING HER! PASSION HAD WELLED IN GREAT FLAMELIKE LEAPS, AND WITHIN HER BREAST THE RHYTHM OF HER PULSE HAD SEEMED AS LOUD AND RAPID AS A DRUMROLL. BE STILL, MY HEART! SHE RECALLED THINKING. BE STILL, LEST YOU BETRAY HOW MUCH I ADORE AND DESIRE HIM!

"Flash, Flash—dash and thrash! Thrash, thrash—thrash that trash!"

But he wasn't thrashing it, not any more. His quality level was still good, and across the Line he was still sitting hunched sideways over his typewriter in the characteristic Garbowitz pose, his thick fingers bludgeoning the keys, smoke from his premature Victory Cigar half-obscuring his shaggy head; but he was losing speed, winding down like an old chronometer. All through the first half and most of the third quarter, his pulp had raced out across the board with the blinding speed that had given him his nickname; now it came stuttering out, with two- or three-second pauses between sentences and longer gaps between paragraphs.

I had already begun refiring my own prose, even as I scanned the Flash's printout, and the detached, noncreative part of my mind thought: I'm going to beat him, no doubt about it now. I'm going to beat him, I'm going to win.

It wasn't a new thought, a sudden realization. I had

known all along that was how it would turn out—a feeling of inevitability, of fate walking on my side of the street. I'd known it even after Ollie Garbowitz won the coin toss and selected MEDICAL ROMANCE, a much easier plot topic than the alternate choice, BLAZING WESTERN ACTION; even after he got off to his usual smoking start and used strings of adjectives to build up a 150-word lead near the end of the first quarter; even after his lead reached 225 words at the opening of the second period, when I pulled an already tender hamstring as I rushed out to the Line after Fueling up and was forced to take a twenty-second injury penalty.

If anything, I had been more confident than ever when the second half began. And that was when the tide had begun to turn in my favor. I'd made up the deficit midway through the third two-thousand-word block, on bursts of speed and one scampering thirty-two-line metaphor that had the crowd on its feet. My resurgence had unnerved the Flash, caused his concentration to waver; just after I drew even, the Head Editor had unfurled two costly penalty flags on him, the pink-and-brown one for Improper Syntax and the green-and-black one for Unacceptable Phrasing. After that there was no way I was about to falter or look back again.

ARABELLA WAITED QUIETLY FOR THE END TO COME. SHE KNEW SHE HAD LOST THE DOCTOR TO VOLUPTUOUS LILLIAN, KNEW THAT HORST WOULD MARRY JANET AND THAT EDWARD AND LUCAS WOULD SOON GO AWAY TO STUDY MEDICINE AT THE SORBONNE. THERE WAS STILL HAROLD, OF COURSE—BUT HE WAS IN LOVE WITH BARBARA, AND MARILYN WOULD SEE TO HIS NEEDS IN ANY CASE. UNLESS PHILIP AND RICHARD HAD MARILYN'S MOTHER COMMITTED TO THE SANITARIUM AGAIN, WHERE YOUNG DOCTOR ASHCRAFT COULD RESUME TREATMENT FOR HER ALCOHOLISM.

"Don't crash, Flash! Thrash that trash!"

THE MARSHAL HOLSTERED HIS SMOKING PIS-TOL, MOSEYED OVER TO WHERE THE BLACKJACK

KID LAY SPRAWLED AND TURNED HIM OVER WITH THE TOE OF ONE BOOT. THE KID WOULD NEVER ROB ANOTHER STAGECOACH, NEVER CHEAT AN-OTHER MAN AT CARDS, NEVER VIOLATE ANOTHER INDIAN SQUAW. HE HAD LIVED BY THE SIX-SHOOTER AND NOW HE HAD DIED BY THE SIX-SHOOTER. IT WAS ONLY FIT AND PROPER, THE MARSHAL THOUGHT AS HE SHIFTED HIS QUID OF TOBACCO FROM ONE LEAN TANNED CHEEK TO THE OTHER. AFTER ALL, THAT WAS THE CODE OF THE WEST.

"Sackett! Sackett! Sackett!"

The Boosters were all standing now, cheering thunderously, filling the Ultradome with the booming sound of my name. Emotion climbed inside me, closed my throat for a couple of seconds. Because I knew Sally would be leading those cheers—sweet wonderful Sally—and that Mom and Dad, and Mort Morgandahl, would be yelling the loudest of all.

I had a sharp mental image of Sally in her red-and-white sweater with the big S on the front. Then one of Mort, with his big wide grin and his shrewd agent's eyes. And of Mom, her rosy cheeks glistening and her hair flashing silver in the lights; and Dad, his stoic Informational technician's face and tough wiry body hiding the biggest heart in the world. They were the four people I cared most about—the four people who were most responsible for my being here today. Without them there just wouldn't have been a pulpeteer known as The Metaphor Kid.

SACKETT 7845, GARBOWITZ 7697.

A hundred and fifty-five words left now, that was all. Just a hundred and fifty-five and all the months in the Junior Creative League and then in the pro Historical Adventure League, all the grueling hours of practice and fitness conditioning, all the visions of fame and wealth and glory would come true. Just a hundred and fifty-five words and I'd have reached the plateau that every prosemaker dreams of reaching from the time he walks out on a field for his first face-off.

The Prose Bowl.

The Prose Bowl!

THEN CARRIE ADAMS, THE LOVELY SCHOOL-
MARM, WAS IN THE MARSHAL'S ARMS AND GAZING
UP AT HIM WITH WORSHIPING EYES.

My pipe had gone out and I typed the last six words of
that sentence with my left hand, while I snaked my right hand
out, caught up my laserflame lighter, and relit the tobacco.
The fans had seen me do that before; it was a trick I had
mastered over the years, not to show off but to save time in
pressure situations, when I needed the good hot smoke from
Virginia burley in my lungs. But this time the maneuver
brought them out of their seats, clapping wildly, and kept
them standing along with the Boosters as I resumed my two-
handed attack on the keyboard.

"OH, RINGO," SHE WHISPERED, "I WAS SO
AFRAID YOU'D BE THE ONE WHO WAS KILLED! I
SHOULD HAVE KNOWN YOU WERE MORE OF A MAN
THAN THE KID. CAN YOU EVER FORGIVE ME FOR
THE WAY I ACTED LAST NIGHT, THE THINGS I SAID?"

Carriage return, tab key.

"Sackett! Sackett! Sackett!"

The whole crowd seemed to be screaming the word now,
caught up in the excitement of these last few seconds. Seventy
thousand people chanting in unison that way, chanting *your*
name, is an awesome thing; it sent little thrills through me,
made me pause again to savor the moment. And to glance
once more at the great numerals that seemed to hang burning
from the stadium dome.

SACKETT 7908, GARBOWITZ 7724.

And then, all at once, the collective voice of the throng
shifted and rose into a shrieking, deafening cheer; the burst of
applause that followed was like a thunderclap. It took me a
second to realize what had happened: The Flash had left his
typewriter and was walking toward the Line—a seldom-seen
gesture of capitulation and defeat. He stopped there and stood

8

waiting for me to end it, waiting with his head held high and the last words he would write this season forming a fiery background above the blur of color and faces beyond.

YES, ARABELLA THOUGHT, THE END HAS COME. AND SO HAS THE TIME FOR THE DROWNING OF SORROWS. A DRINK SEEMS TO BE IN ORDER—SEVERAL DRINKS, IN FACT, ALONE IN A DARK ROOM. AT A TIME LIKE THIS, WHAT ELSE IS THERE TO DO EXCEPT TO GET QUIETLY FUELED?

A few fans were already trying to run out onto the field; the security Servos went after them, blowing their ultrasonic directional whistles and brandishing tranq weapons. But I scarcely noticed. My eyes were back on my typewriter and my mind was intent again on only one thing: punching out those last few words that would bring me to victory.

"YOU'RE FORGIVEN, MISS CARRIE," THE MARSHAL DRAWLED. HE LOOKED AROUND AT THE OTHER TOWNSFOLK WHO HAD COME OUT TO GATHER NEARBY, SAW RELIEF INSTEAD OF FEAR IN THEIR FACES, ACCEPTANCE INSTEAD OF HOSTILITY. "AND SO'S THE REST OF CIMARRON CITY," HE SAID. "A GRUDGE IS A MIGHTY HEAVY THING. I RECKON MY GUN AND MY BADGE ARE MORE'N ENOUGH FOR ONE MAN TO CARRY."

Another glance at the scoreboard.

Word count at 7972.

"The Prose Bowl for Sackett! The Prose Bowl for Sackett! The Prose Bowl for Sackett!"

AND WITH THAT, THE MARSHAL TOOK CARRIE'S HAND AND TOGETHER THEY WALKED THROUGH THE TOWN HE HAD FOUGHT AND TAMED, THE TOWN HE WOULD CALL HOME AT LAST.

There was bedlam in the Ultradome as I typed the words THE END and the Head Editor declared the Face-Off officially ended with a wave of his star-spangled Prose Bowl flag. People were pouring out of the stands, milling about everywhere; the security Servos were on the turf in force, more than two hundred of them forming a protective ring around the center-field area. Everyone seemed to be screaming at the top of his voice, and the Sackett and Garbowitz bands were playing at full volume; the voice of the P.A. announcer was all but drowned out by the din as he gave the final score: The Metaphor Kid 8000, the Kansas City Flash 7758.

Half the TriDim cameras mounted on the dome rafters seemed to be panning the confusion of bodies, but the other half were homed in on me, I knew, for a series of post-game closeups. When I stood from my machine, lifting my arms in the traditional victory salute, I could feel myself smiling so hard and so wide that my jaw muscles ached. I had never been happier or more proud than I was right at this moment.

Then I saw the Flash coming toward me, and I lowered my arms and limped over to meet him, favoring my injured leg. We clasped hands, touched forearms and elbows to let the TriDim fans know there hadn't been any grudge element in the match. Garbowitz was still standing tall and proud, but you could see how tired he was and how much losing the Face-Off had affected him; in his eyes there was sadness and the pain of defeat. And something else, too, something that I'd seen in the eyes of a lot of old pros like the Flash—and not just when they'd lost, either. It was almost a sense of personal tragedy, or maybe a bitter emptiness, or maybe something else altogether; I just couldn't quite define it or understand it. Maybe it had something to do with advancing age or how many face-offs you'd been in and how many years you played in the Bigs. I hope it never happened to me, whatever it was. But I didn't think it would. I couldn't imagine myself being empty or torn up inside by some sort of affliction.

"You wrote a hell of a game today, kid," the Flash said when he released my hand. "The way you were cranking in the second half, there isn't a pulpeteer in the business who could have matched you."

"I guess it just all came together for me at the right time," I said. "I thought I was done for when I pulled my hamstring."

"Don't be modest, kid. You knew all along you could beat me; I could tell just by looking at you. You're good, damn good—better than I was at your age." That odd something flickered in his eyes again, seemed to make him wince. "For your sake I hope—"

"You hope what, Flash?"

"Never mind. And don't call me Flash," he said. "My name is Ollie. Kansas City Flash is a name the media gave me, just like they made you The Metaphor Kid. They paste those damn names on us like labels, but we don't have to do it to ourselves."

"Okay, Ollie. Sorry."

"Forget it. Well, here's luck in the Prose Bowl."

"Thanks," I said. "I'll do the best I can."

"Sure you will. Scuff him, whoever you play."

"If he doesn't scuff me first."

The Flash nodded and moved away in a stiff gait to where his Servos were waiting with containers of Fuel. My own Servos had gathered nearby, I realized, and they were shouting, "We're Number One! We're Number One!" I went over and embraced each of them, because I wouldn't see them again after today; I'd be assigned a new team of Servos in the Prose Bowl. And one pressed one of my own Fuel containers, already open and inviting, into my hand.

I took a three-ounce victory shot and it worked its magic right away; I could feel myself loosening up inside, the knots of tension every pro suffers in major competition starting to unravel. Three more ounces soothed me out nicely—added a different glow to the glow of triumph, softened the shrieks of the fans and the brassy tempo of the band music. I was all set now for the first of the post-game interviews, the on-field spot with one of the TriDim announcers.

But there wasn't going to be an on-field interview, it turned out. One of the Assistant Line Editors, a burly red-haired man named Huxtable, came running over with word that the spot had been canceled for security reasons because of the unruly crowd; they wanted me off the field and into my designated locker room, and the rest of the playing area completely cleared, as soon as possible. Ever since half a dozen prosemakers had been mauled in crowd flareups in the tough and vicious Quality Lit League three years ago, and Fantasy Fats McGee had been killed by a flying Fuel container after losing a quarterfinal match that same year, the League Editors and the rest of the officials were safety-conscious. Some said they didn't care half as much about the well-being of the pulpeteers as they did about their own reputations and the money they were making, but I didn't believe that myself.

A phalanx of security Servos, their tranq weapons drawn and ready, began to escort me toward the east-side tunnel. Huxtable walked along at my side. We were halfway to the tunnel, in the middle of the slow-moving wedge, when he leaned over close and spoke in confidential tones.

"Can we get together later today, Sackett?"

"Get together?"

"There's something I want to talk over with you—something very important."

"What is it?"

"I don't have time to go into it here," Huxtable said. "It has to do with you going to the Prose Bowl and it's a little complicated. But it could mean a lot of money for you."

"Some sort of endorsement?"

"Investment might be a better word. How about if I meet you for a few minutes in the Fuel lounge at your Complex? Say nineteen hundred hours, before the West Coast semifinal comes on TriDim?"

I hesitated. "Well, I don't know," I said. "I don't want to miss any of the Face-Off . . ."

"You won't. Fifteen minutes is all it'll take."

"Does it have to be tonight?"

"Afraid so. This can't wait."

I didn't know Huxtable very well, or much about him except that he'd been a pulpeteer himself in the semipros and for one mediocre season in the Soft-Core Porn League before becoming an Assistant Editor (a position that was little more than that of a Servo). But he seemed friendly enough, and a prosemaker can't afford to pass up any decent opportunity to invest in his future, even when he's at or near the top like I was now; the competition in all the leagues is fierce and the average pro career is less than ten years. Besides, Sally and I were planning to get married right after the season ended— and we both wanted kids, now that the birth restrictions had been modified.

"Okay, then," I said to Huxtable. "Nineteen-hundred hours in the Fuel lounge at my Complex."

"Good kid. Nice scuffing today, by the way."

"Thanks."

He dropped back and left me to wonder just what sort of investment deal he had in mind. Something to do with Luna Colony, probably, I thought. That was where all the smart money was these days.

But then I stopped thinking about Huxtable, about investments, because we had reached the tunnel and the fans there began showering us—showering me—with flowers and chanting my name again. I raised my Fuel container to them, to show my appreciation, and then took a small swallow. More flowers rained down in approval. Today those flowers were carnations, red and white, the Sackett colors; but next week they would be roses. Red and white roses.

Next week—in the Prose Bowl.

2

The first thing I did when I entered my locker room was to strip off my sweat-damp uniform and slip into the Body-Ease unit. I had fifteen minutes before the TriDim interviews and the post-game press conference, and I wanted to look my best—not for the media but for Sally and Mom and Dad, who would be watching and waiting for me afterward. Mort Morgandahl would be with me for the interviews, the way he always was, to keep things moving along and the scribes from getting too personal or too nasty. He was due any time now; his first chore after any match was to make sure Sally and the folks got out of harm's way.

While the Body-Ease massaged my sore leg, administered a thermoshower and then dried and deodorized me, I let myself think about the Prose Bowl for the first time. I hadn't dared project ahead before now, not with an opponent as tough and wily as the Kansas City Flash to overcome first. "One at a time, Rex," Mort had told me early on in my career. "Always take your face-offs one at a time."

Who would I be facing across the Line next Sunday? Who would my adversary be out there in Greater Los Angeles, in the famous and crumbling Coliseum, the last of the open-air Old-Sport stadiums? Fast-Action Eddie Duke? Or the grand old man of New-Sport, Leon Culp, better known as The Cranker? Which one of them would win the West Coast semifinal tonight in the Las Vegas New-Sport Arena?

Well, I knew which one I *wanted* it to be. I'd maintained a neutral pose when the media asked me who I preferred to face-off against, but deep down inside I was pulling for The Cranker. He was fifty-seven years old now, and in a career spanning almost four full decades he had punched out more than twenty million words in nearly a thousand matches; and he'd been my idol ever since Dad took me to see my first pro game when I was ten—the almost lengendary confrontation between The Cranker and Three-Finger Luke Waddell, in the old Metro Stadium back in '37. Culp's two-word victory with an incredible last-ditch sixty-line simile was the most exciting thing I'd ever seen in my life.

It was true that The Cranker had never made it to the Prose Bowl; the closest he'd ever come were a pair of defeats in the quarterfinals and a close loss to The Hackensack Hack, the eventual champion, in the semis three years ago. And there were some who said that he couldn't win the big ones; that he depended too much on the Fuel now to get him through the tougher face-offs; that he was pretty near washed up and had made it this far only because of weak competition in his Mainstream Commercial Fic League and in the play-offs. The consensus was that he didn't stand much of a chance against Fast-Action Eddie. A few of the younger scribes were even predicting a thousand-word scuff.

But that wasn't the way I saw it, not any of it. As far as I was concerned, nobody knew more about the business or about twentieth-century prose than Leon Culp, and when he was on top of his game nobody could equal him behind a machine. He was the best there was, it was as simple as that. And I wanted to go up against the best, to beat the best if I could, just the way I had beaten the Kansas City Flash this afternoon.

I was putting on a clean jersey—they expected you to come in uniform to the TriDim and press interviews—when a rapping sounded on the door and Mort Morgandahl came in. He was wearing a purple Edwardian coat, a yellow-silk Space Academy tunic, a Phi Beta Kappa key, and tailored white wool chaps. Mort handles a lot of pulpeteers in all the different New-Sport leagues and he always dresses a little flamboyantly, to impress this client or that one. The Edwardian was in honor of me and my prowess in the Historical Adventure League; there was no telling who he was spiffing for in the Futuristic Fic, Quality Lit, and Horse Opera leagues.

He threw his arms around me, saying, "Way to scuff, kid, way to scuff!"

"I felt good out there in the second half, Mort. Real good."

"And you looked good, too. Had us worried for a while when you hurt your leg; but when you punched out that thirty-two-liner we knew you couldn't lose."

"Sally and the folks okay?"

"Sure. They can't wait to see you."

"I can't wait to see them either."

"It won't be long, kid," Mort said. "Listen, how's the hamstring feel? Still sore?"

"Not too bad now. The Body-Ease took out most of the pain."

"Well, work on it during the week, all right? Do a little running on the old Exerciser. We can't have it giving you any trouble next Sunday. Not *next* Sunday."

"It won't, Mort, don't worry."

We stood looking at each other for ten seconds or so; then we both grinned and started to laugh. And pretty soon we grabbed hold of each other and danced around the locker room like a couple of Fueled fans, both of us shouting the same thing over and over: "The Prose Bowl! We're going to the Prose Bowl!"

I had to stop before long because my leg began to give out twinges and I was afraid of straining the hamstring again. Mort suggested we have a shot of Fuel before we went down to the Media Hall, just to loosen up for the interviews, and we did. Then we had another one for luck.

When we got to the Hall a pair of Servos escorted us in to where the TriDim cameras and announcers were waiting.

Outside in the stadium proper I could hear singing and cheering: Some of the fans had stayed on, maybe even to catch a glimpse of The Metaphor Kid on his way out of the Ultradome and into the Prose Bowl. The thought made me start grinning all over again.

The New-Sport announcers were Harmon Penn and Vinnie Winkle. Winkle was a former pulpeteer and one of the best word-by-word men in the New-Sport game; Penn was the chief "color commentator" on the National TriDim Network, but he was also pompous, egocentric, nasty-minded, and not very well informed. Nobody knew where he'd come from or just what his credentials were for the job. All of the other announcers had been prosemakers themselves, or had worked as agents or Editors; some, like Winkle, had even gotten close to the top in their respective leagues. But so far as anybody knew, Penn had never been at even the bottom levels of competition. He was always vague on his background anyway, but he spoke with such authority, and even though he was wrong about a third of the time, the other announcers were afraid to challenge him. Maybe the reason he'd gotten the top commentator's job, I'd once said to Mort, was precisely because he *hadn't* played New-Sport. Like 95 percent of the public he knew next to nothing about the intricacies of wordsmithing, so maybe it was that negative quality the fans were able to identify with. Anyhow, I didn't like him at all. None of us pros did.

Penn didn't say anything to Mort or me when we came in. He just stood glaring the way he does, all sour-faced and gimlet-eyed, which makes him look like a sort of evil Santa Claus because he has a round, red face and a round belly and powdered, silvery hair. Winkle, though, was all smiles and full of congratulations as he showed us to our places. Then the cameras were ready, and just before they started to roll Penn moved in and took a position that favored him as the dominant member of the announcing team. Winkle didn't like that; you could tell by his expression. But he didn't say or do anything about it.

It was Winkle who made the introductory comments and asked the first few questions: How did I feel? Was my leg hurting and did I think it would bother me next Sunday? Was I excited about my first appearance in the Prose Bowl? Did I consider the Flash to be the toughest opponent I'd faced so far in the play-offs? When did I first begin to feel I had the match won? I was a little nervous at first, even with the Fuel working inside me; I always did think my best and feel the most confident when I was behind a typewriter. But Winkle was friendly enough and didn't prod me, and Mort helped me over the rough spots, so that I didn't embarrass myself.

"I thought you got off some really good lines today, Metaphor," Winkle said then. "I especially liked the one early in the third quarter, when the Marshal is riding out into the desert to find the old prospector. 'It was as if he were riding into a strange land, some mythical kingdom of weird shapes, majestic spires, and saw-toothed bluffs like the jagged teeth of a terrible monster.' Real poetic. Real metaphoric."

"Well," I said modestly, feeling much more at ease now, almost relaxed, "well, you know how it is, Vinnie. When you're cranking fast and hard, sometimes you can reach back for that little extra you didn't even know you had."

"Is that so?" Penn said. "I rather doubt it. Contrary to the opinion of my esteemed colleague Mr. Winkle, *I* thought your prose was anything but poetic and metaphorical. Contrived would be a better term. Weak, prosaic, watered-down. Junior Creative League writing at its most mundane."

It was the first time Penn had spoken since the interview began and it jarred me pretty hard. That's the way he does it: He holds back, waiting for the right psychological moment, and then he jumps on you and starts to carve you up with his fancy words. I'd seen him do it dozens of times on TriDim, and Mort had warned me about it on the way down from the locker room, but it still caught me off guard.

"What?" I said. "What?"

"You heard me, Rex," Penn said in his silky voice. "You

had your way today, there's no denying that. But if the Flash hadn't been off his game, it might have been a much different story."

I didn't know what to say; I felt all tongue-tied with rising anger. But Mort stepped forward and snapped, "It didn't look to me or to anyone in the stands that either the Flash *or* Rex was off his game; I'll bet it didn't look that way to any of the fans on TriDim either."

"Be that as it may. The fact is, your client's ineffectual prose and general padding were noticeable to any qualified observer such as myself who cared to analyze them for what they were."

"Ineffectual prose?" I said. "General padding?"

"Not to mention the strings of clichés."

"Clichés?" I said. "Now wait a minute—"

Mort touched my arm, a signal between us that I should keep quiet and let him handle things. But I could see that he was almost as angry now as I was. So was Winkle, for that matter, but he still wasn't about to challenge Penn; he just stood there looking half-humiliated and half-bewildered.

"I've checked with the Head Editor and the Line Editor, among others," Penn said. "The consensus is that Sackett produced quite a bit of extraneous material—quite a bit. Now Blazing Western Action is wide open, if I may coin a phrase, for both padding and strings of clichés, but what if your client should draw a plot topic in the Prose Bowl which demands elisions, compression?"

"Like what?" I said.

"Suspense Fic, for example."

"Rex has terrific range," Mort said. "There isn't any kind of pulp he can't write with the best in any league. He wouldn't be here today if he wasn't strong in *all* the categories. You ought to know that as well as anybody, Penn, as long as you've been following New-Sport."

"Agents are optimistic by definition," Penn said with one of his nasty little smiles. He looked at me. "How about it, Rex? Do you feel you're proficient in all the categories?"

"Sure I do," I said. "I never had any trouble with Suspense Fic or anything else—"

"Then you don't believe the pressure will bother you next Sunday?"

"Pressure? What pressure?"

"The pressure of trying to produce prose that isn't padded, cliché-ridden, amateurish, and ineffectual while going up against either Fast-Action Eddie Duke or The Cranker, two of the premier pulpeteers in the history of New-Sport."

I could feel myself starting to sputter. Mort started to say something, but Penn's knives-in-velvet voice overrode him.

"Now about your hamstring, Rex," he said to me. "This is the first injury you've ever sustained in competition, isn't that right?"

"That's right. But—"

"Don't you think it came at a propitious time?"

"Propitious?"

"Isn't there some relevance to the fact that you sustained an injury in the semifinal match? That perhaps it shows a certain weakness in your physical makeup to coincide with the weakness in your prosemaking abilities?"

Those questions got to Mort as much as they did to me. He groped blindly into the pocket of his Edwardian, took out a whitish Complex pass card, and waved it in Penn's face; it was the kind of thing he always did when he got really upset. "We don't have to listen to any more of your abuse," he said. "You got no right to infer that Rex can't stand up to the strain."

Penn smiled again. "If the doublet fits, you have to wear it. To coin a phrase."

The anger was boiling inside me and I wanted to say something nasty and cutting of my own about Penn's sex life, which I'd heard some of the other pulpeteers speculating on and which everybody agreed had to be as repellent as he was. But then I thought of the millions of fans watching at this moment, and what I'd gone through and what lay ahead of me and what I owed all of them, not to mention Mort and Sally and the folks, and I bit my tongue and held back. Penn's technique was to get you to lose your temper, after which he would say that pulpeteers were just a bunch of neurotics anyway, shaky and unstable athletes, no models for the general population, highly overrated, and so on.

"The interview is over," Mort was saying. "Rex is very tired; he's had a difficult day and he wants to be with his family."

Winkle, looking relieved, started to say something by way of a sign-off; but Penn cut him off. "One more question. Metaphor, tell the truth now: Do you honestly feel you stand a chance in the Prose Bowl?"

"What kind of question is that?" Mort said.

"A twenty-four-year-old kid against either Fast-Action Eddie Duke or Leon Culp? Seriously, now—it looks like a mismatch to me."

"I think my chances are just fine," I snapped.

"The old confidence, eh?" Penn said. "Ah, but what happens if the hamstring goes again? If you aren't able to pad, if the clichés won't come in sufficient quantity, if—"

I made a little sound in my throat and took a step forward, and I don't know what would have happened then if Mort hadn't grabbed my shoulder and pulled me away. Penn was smiling all over his fat face, looking very pleased with himself, as Winkle signed off and the cameras quit rolling; he hadn't even flinched when I started for him. Maybe he'd have liked it if I had hit him—and not just because it would have given him plenty to talk about on his next TriDim cast. If the other pulpeteers were right about his sex life, getting hit was just one of the things he enjoyed.

"Don't let that bastard get to you," Mort said as we headed in for the press conference. "Don't take his crap personally, kid."

But I *was* taking it personally. Penn hadn't just upset me with his vicious remarks, he'd taken away some of the glow of my victory over the Flash, robbed me of some of my excitement at being in the Prose Bowl. It was almost like a violation, what he'd done to me—a physical attack not on me as an athlete but as a human being.

Why did there have to be men like him in New-Sport? Why did there have to be people who didn't know anything about the business, or care anything about it either, who tried to spoil things for the pulpeteers? Prosemaking was tough enough as it was; why couldn't the Penns leave us alone?

I said all of that to Mort, just before we entered the Press Room. "Just keep calm," he told me. "It's the Penns who fade away to oblivion, not the Sacketts. That's what you've got to remember."

"Sure," I said, even though that wasn't really true. It was usually the wordsmiths who faded away; Penn had been at his job for at least a decade. Even the greatest of us lasted not much more than ten years: There weren't many like The Cranker, who had been at or near the top for thirty years. Of the reigning league champions when I had come in six scant years ago, the only one still active was Culp himself. It was a young person's game, mostly a man's game, Penn reminded us often enough; it took a kind of physical stamina, raw creativeness, and energy that were very hard to maintain. Maybe that was one of the reasons why only two women had reached even the quarterfinals since the beginning of New-Sport—Kate Day, The Kentucy Knuckler; and Junk Artist Jenny—and why one had never been in the Prose Bowl. Women physically couldn't stand up to the pressure, the strain, the Fuel intake which was almost a requirement of the game. Then, too, just as women for unexplainable reasons had never seemed to get to the top levels of Old-Sport chess, none of them having even competed for a world championship in over two hundred years, so might there be something absent in their genetic equipment which kept them from becoming powerful competitive forces in New-Sport. (Some missing "cell of greatness," Penn had once said in his ugly way, inciting protests from women's groups which he had totally ignored.)

That need for physical stamina and expanding Fuel capacity was already giving *me* long thoughts, as young as I was, as to how long even I would be able to last. Not that I was all that worried, though; I was pretty certain it would be quite a while before I was through. And I sure hadn't come this far to lose the Prose Bowl or my career at this stage because of some minor problem like a hamstring pull. I intended to be around long enough to secure my future and to enjoy my success.

If only the Penns will let me, I thought.

If only they'll *let* me.

3

The press conference was a lot smoother and easier than the TriDim interview; most of the questions from the fifty or sixty New-Sport scribes were straightforward and fair, and the few personal ones Mort handled without any problem. It lasted just under an hour. Which was a good thing because I was so tired and Fueled out and anxious to see Sally and the folks by then that I couldn't have lasted much longer under those hot lights and probing questions.

When we finally came into the Family Hall, seeing the smiling faces of the three people I loved most in the world restored some of my energy and all of my good spirits. Dad smacked me on the shoulder and told me he'd known from the first, the very first when I began spelling out words to myself in my crib, that I would be a New-Sport champion. And Mom cried a little and ruffled my hair and I hugged her good and hard. But it was Sally I hugged the longest, nuzzling her silky blond hair while she cuddled against me and told me how proud she was.

I had known Sally ever since we were kids, and we'd been what I guess you'd call sweethearts for ten years; but it was only the last year or so that we'd definitely decided to get married once this season was over. But when it became apparent to both Mort and me that this was going to be my year in the Historical Adventure League, maybe my year to go all the way in the play-offs and into the Prose Bowl, Mort had persuaded me to hold off on any kind of preparations for the wedding so I could dedicate my full time to prosemaking. Sally hadn't been too pleased at my decision because she knew it would mean spending almost no time with her. And she was right, much as I hated to have it happen. She went along gamely enough, though, because that's the kind of person she is. Of course, she did have a tendency to complain now and then, particularly about the total commitment of a pulpeteer to his prosemaking and what that commitment might do to him later on in life, but Mort assured me that was chronic among all the wives and girlfriends of established pros. From what I'd seen in my limited experience, he was absolutely right.

We all left the Ultradome together, escorted by the security Servos to make sure we weren't mugged or bothered on our way to the stadium aircab station. It was just three days before Year Day and the weather was very cold, threatening one of those heavy snows the New York megalopolis gets late in December and throughout January. It was good to get inside the heated aircab, although I don't usually mind the cold too much. And good to be on the way back to my Complex in Outer Greenwich Village to celebrate my victory. The party was Mort's idea and he'd originally wanted to have it at his brand-new pink Sky Complex; but another new building was going up nearby and the twenty-four-hour construction created a terrific din. It was just as well. I was too tired to want to do much traveling around tonight.

As we whisked above the mazelike streets and the glittering Informationals and the seemingly endless rows of Sky Complexes hurled upward beyond the cloudline, I sat with my arm around Sally so I could kiss her and tell her how much I loved her. We were alone, too—Mom and Dad had gone with Mort in another aircab—or I couldn't have done any of that private lovemaking. Not in front of the folks under *any* circumstances.

Sally and I had made a decision a long time ago: We

were not going to do any lovemaking at all until we were married. This put us in the minority; going to bed together is more or less what being engaged is all about. But we tended to take lovemaking a lot more seriously than most people and didn't want to dishonor our feelings by doing it out of wedlock. Which isn't the way a lot of folks feel nowadays, as I said, and from what I hear it isn't at all the way things are outside the megalopolises—only you have to make your own choices. Like Dad says: You don't live for society, you live for yourself.

Things have loosened up a great deal in the past twenty years or so, that's for sure. Lovemaking out of wedlock was illegal for a while after the millenia; the government banned it as part of the Reconstruction following the Crash of 2006. But by 2025 it wasn't thought of as being all that serious—not nearly as serious as counterfeiting a Fuel ration card, for instance—and although it's still illegal under the statutes, nobody pays much attention to it as long as it's kept quiet. I suspect that nowadays we're in the last generation of people like me and Sally who are still solemn about the law and personal honor, and in ten years or so lovemaking out of wedlock will again be part of the norms of society, as it was back in the latter half of the twentieth century.

I tend to think a lot about the present and the future, and so I also tend to think about the past a lot too. History fascinates me, and not just because I do my cranking in the Historical Adventure League. For one thing it explains the present and why things are the way they are. Mort once said I think too much about *everything*, but thinking is really a necessary tool for the successful pulpeteer. So I figure I ought to do it every chance I get.

Anyhow, Sally and I really needed those few minutes of privacy in the aircab. And deserved them too. We did argue a little bit toward the end of the trip, the way we have before, but it wasn't anything serious. She thinks that win or lose I ought to get out of competition after the Prose Bowl, that we should even consider relocating to Luna Colony. It's a ridiculous idea, only I just can't seem to make her see it that way.

"You don't understand what the Prose Bowl could mean for us," I said to her. "It's not something you can just *leave* as a champion, or even as the defeated challenger. There's an honored tradition you have to uphold."

"What honored tradition?" Sally said. She's a very intelligent woman but she really doesn't understand the business, as only those of us who are pulpeteers can. "Rex, you're going to have to retire sooner or later, you know that. So why not sooner?"

"Because I have an obligation," I said.

"To whom?"

"To Mort, to all the fans, to the other prosemakers. How would it look if I just walked away—if I just *quit?* I'm not a quitter, Sally, and I couldn't stand for people to think of me that way."

"Which is more important?" She asked in her reasonable, levelheaded way. "How people think of you or your own happiness? *Our* happiness, the future of our"—she lowered her eyes demurely—"our children."

"We're more important," I said, "but . . ."

"But what?"

"Sally, I'm a pulpeteer."

"You're also a man named Rex Sackett," she said. "It's Rex Sackett I'm in love with, not The Metaphor Kid—"

She seemed to want to say something else, but the aircab had arrived at the rooftop station on my dark-blue Complex and was settling to a halt, the doors starting to glide open. Outside, in New York's perpetual haze, I could see that Mort and the folks were already there and waiting on the platform. A few other people were waiting there too—neighbors, Servos, a couple of scribes.

There were some cheers as Sally and I stepped out of the cab, and I had to shake hands all around and answer a few more questions about the Face-Off before we could push through to the entrance. One of the Servos on duty there took my dark-blue pass card—all Complex pass cards are color-coded in New York, at least in the better neighborhoods like mine—and slid it into the Checkpoint computer, which scanned my dental patterns and fingerprints and toeprints to make sure I was a legitimate resident. Mom and Dad and Mort were registered as qualified guests, so it only took a few seconds for their guest cards to scan through. Then we were all inside and in the chute heading down to the 197th floor.

My apartment was one of the nicer ones in the Complex, even though it was on a lower floor: three rooms, counting the bathroom, and all the modern servomechanisms allowed by law, including the best TriDim on the market. I also had it furnished nice and comfortable, with twentieth-century prose posters on the walls and old-fashioned typewriters and other artifacts that I'd begun to collect arranged here and there. I think it's a great place and I don't want to give it up, but Sally keeps insisting we find a new apartment in a new Complex after we're married, one that'll satisfy both our tastes. Starting fresh, she calls it. Blending interests and life-styles, she says. But I don't know. What she likes is music-related stuff, old instruments and things. That's because she has a part-time job as a Musicological Researcher and Recoverer and takes it very seriously; she claims it's every bit as important as being a pulpeteer. Which is nonsense. As far as I'm concerned, Musicological Researcher and Recoverer is just a fancy label for Servo. And I never did much like music anyway. So I'm not so sure this blending-interests-and-life-styles idea of hers is going to work out, although I guess I'm willing to try it for her sake.

After I finished security-locking the door, I sat down on the contour-form couch next to Sally. Mort folded himself into a long-chair and lit one of the cheroots he likes. Dad went about setting up a container of Fuel and Mom began arranging a few special snacks she'd brought up for the celebration earlier.

I watched the folks at work and thought that they were

the best parents anyone could ever have. They've never asked a thing of me other than that I do my best. "Be the best version of yourself" is how Dad always put it. But sometimes they kind of made me feel a little guilty, because it's impossible for them to understand what my life is like or what I need to do with it.

Like my Dad, for instance. He's an Assignment Supervisor for one of the bigger Informational agencies, which means that he goes out with a technical crew three days a week and takes down old Informationals and puts up new ones—signs warning against pedestrianism on the traffic ways, signs recruiting for Luna Colony, signs for this consumer product or that public utility, signs for just about anything you can think of.

Informationals are the biggest business, at least in terms of actual employment, that there is today. It isn't the making of products that is important anymore because that's all done by machines, and it isn't the differences between the products because there really isn't any; Quasi-Fuel is Quasi-Fuel, for example, and that's all it is. The Informationals persuade people to use this commodity instead of that one and so on, and working with them is a powerful and important job, as Dad used to point out to me, because without Informationals people would just buy without selectivity and perfectly good manufacturers would go out of business, which would only add to the Servo problem. As it is, free enterprise is maintained and neither the manufacturer nor the consumer has to suffer because everything's the same.

Dad's a pretty bright guy, I always thought, but his problem is he can't read. He was one of the post-institutional generation just before the literacy tables got turned around, and the idea of being reschooled or even admitting to anyone that he needed reschooling was hard for him, so he just didn't bother. To this day he won't really admit that he can't read anything except simple Informationals; I found out about it from Mom. It's kind of sad when he comments on all the New-

Sport competitions and tells me how much he enjoys my prose without ever getting into the specifics.

Mom can read a little but she doesn't enjoy it. She thinks reading is dangerous, at best that it's a waste of time: Everything we need to know, she says, we're taught by the TriDim broadcasts. That's kind of sad too, I guess.

Sometimes I wonder how I was able to learn to read so easily, coming from the kind of environment I did. How I was able to involve myself so deeply, at such an early age, in twentieth-century prose that I never wanted to be anything in my life except a pulpeteer. Maybe it was just some sort of genetic quirk; I don't know. Anyway, the folks have always been proud of my abilities and never tried to discourage me in any way, so in the long run I suppose it doesn't matter that they don't understand me and Mom almost always changes the subject when I try to tell her what it's really like out there in a face-off.

Well, the party got underway and it was a nice one for a while. Mort was the center of it, outlining his plans for me—endorsements, celebrity tours, and the like—after I became Prose Bowl champion. And we all ate Mom's snacks and Fueled up, except for Sally who is one of the few people I've ever known who never uses Fuel; she says she doesn't like the fuzzy way it makes her feel. I don't understand that at all, but of course she's entitled to her opinions and to a few little idiosyncracies. I'm pretty broad-minded that way.

But then Mort started talking about how the pressure would be off me after this year and I could take it easy and enjoy the benefits of what I'd accomplished in New-Sport. Mom and Dad smiled and nodded, but Sally sat forward and said, "What do you mean, there won't be any more pressure? He's supposed to defend his championship if he wins, isn't he? And if he loses he's supposed to come back with even more intensity?"

Mort shrugged. "He's not going to lose next week. Are you, Rex?"

"No," I said.

"That's not the point," Sally said. "Whether he wins *or* loses, the pressure will be on him again all next year."

"A year is a long time from now," Mort said.

"I know a year's a long time. Rex and I haven't really been together for almost a year; I know exactly how long it is."

Mort said, "I wouldn't worry about it now. We don't want to distract Rex."

"I'm not trying to distract him; you're the one who is, telling him how wonderful his life will be and how all our troubles will be over if he wins. But look what's happened to the past Prose Bowl champions. Two have suffered Fuel overloads in competition, one died of a heart attack, one had to be committed to an institution for trying to murder an Editor, and one has been struggling to stay out of last place in his own league for the past four seasons."

Dad kind of frowned and said, "That's true. And then there's what happened to Wee-Wristed Wally Gold."

Wee-Wristed Wally Gold had won the Prose Bowl last year, and what had happened to him was that he hadn't even been able to suit up this year in defense of his championship because he'd broken both legs and damaged his spine on Luna in the off-season. He'd been making a celebrity tour and in a moment of exuberance he'd forgotten that he was in a weightless environment. But that was just a freak accident. It didn't mean anything, any more than the fates of the other winners meant anything: None of those things were going to happen to *me*.

I started to say that, but Sally was talking again. "Exactly," she said to Dad. And then, to Mort: "Wally Gold is the only pulpeteer who didn't fail trying to defend his title, and that's only because he's lying in a simulated Earth environment at Luna Colony, not even able to *move*. Is that the kind of future you want Rex to have?"

Mort gave her a keen look. "You know a lot about the business, don't you, Sally?"

"I'm Rex's girl," she said, "so I ought to know everything I can about what he's doing. It doesn't take much research and besides, everybody follows New-Sport; that's what Rex says, anyway."

"I meant about what happened to the champions," Mort said. "Most people don't bother with statistics like those."

"That's because most people don't even think about the champions when the Prose Bowl is over. And once they're no longer champions, people don't think about them at all. It could be even *worse* for Rex if he wins next Sunday than it is now."

Mom was kind of poking Dad by this time, giving him funny looks, and Sally and Mort were staring at each other. I felt a blush beginning to spread all over my face. It's a very uncomfortable thing to sit with your friends and loved ones in your own apartment and feel like an object, some kind of treasured but undependable mechanism that has to be handled in a particular fashion or it'll stop functioning—something like a holographic projector, say, that responds even to changes in humidity by streaking its images and making them appear freakish and grotesque.

"Look," I said to all of them, "why don't you stop talking about me like that? Why don't you just let me work out for myself what's ahead of me? None of you have to go out and write the prose, you know; it's *me* out there behind the machine, all alone."

My voice must have been louder than I'd intended and my manner a little angrier because Mom and Dad seemed to twitch uncomfortably in their chairs and even Sally moved away from me with a hurt expression. Mort's face was set in a way I knew well; the first I'd seen it was when he told me at the beginning of our relationship that I was best qualified for the Historical Adventure League. It was a look that said he knew what was best and he wasn't going to be argued with.

He got to his feet and seemed to loom over the rest of us. "Rex is right," he said. "He's about to enter into the most important competition of his life and we're sitting here picking on him. I think the best thing we can do right now is to leave him alone, let him get some rest."

Nobody disagreed. When he went to open the door Mom and Dad followed right away, looking a little contrite and a little bewildered. Sally followed more slowly, with me beside her, and once we got there she reached out and squeezed my hand in a solemn way.

"Rex," she said, "you're going to have to make some choices very soon. Just you, nobody else. I hope you realize that." Then, before I could say anything, she turned and followed Mom and Dad out into the corridor. She didn't even say good-bye. The folks hadn't either, but that was different, somehow.

Mort and I were left facing each other. "What choices?" I asked him. "What did she mean, Mort?"

"It doesn't matter," he said. "You made all your choices a hell of a long time ago, when you became a pulpeteer. Don't even think about it, kid. Don't think about anything except winning the Prose Bowl next Sunday."

And then he was gone too and I was alone.

I paced through the empty apartment, stared out the window at the megalopolis beyond: the huge network of Sky Complexes and Industrials and flickering Informational signs stretching far away into the mist—two hundred kilometers away to where the barren Rural Lands began, with their population of Outlanders who by custom or by choice lived outside the megalopolises and foraged a life from the earth. In the last half century all the cities had retracted into just a few, and those few had expanded upward as well as outward, so that five-hundred-story towers pierced the sky. Amidst the buildings the streets ran like little capillaries in the subsurface of the body; I'd walked those streets often. But I had only flown above, high above, the great gates that stretched electric at the perimeters.

Sometimes the megalopolis, the entire shape of the country, overwhelms me; I shivered and turned from the window. The thought of being here alone right now didn't appeal to me at all. And then I remembered that I didn't have to stay here alone, at least not for awhile: I'd made an appointment to meet the Assistant Line Editor, Huxtable, downstairs in the Fuel lounge at nineteen hundred hours. I glanced at my chronometer. Nineteen hundred hours was just fifteen minutes from now.

I was out of there and into the chute in three.

4

When I came into the Fuel lounge I used my Unlimited card to order a medium-sized individual container. The place was fairly crowded and I took a lot of envious glances, but at least there weren't any nosy scribes; as important as the semifinal matches are and as much as the media flocks around a prosemaker immediately after the contest ends, they tend to leave us alone again pretty fast. I've never understood why. Mort says it's because there isn't much real celebrity on its own terms in the competitions, but I just don't know.

Part of the envy had to do with my Unlimited Fuel card. Fuel is strictly rationed and has been for several years; the government controls the outflow and the intake through its Distribution Centers and through the ration cards distributed to all adult citizens, the quotas depending on level of accomplishment, age, personal history, criminal record or lack of it, and so on. It's possible to work your way slowly up the social hierarchy, as my dad has, to a Senior card, which permits as many as eight large individual Fuel containers a day; but the unrestricted cards are at a premium, available only to public officials, top Informational executives, persons in important spatial and other research positions, and pulpeteers who have reached the upper levels of competition. If Fuel wasn't tightly controlled, very little work would be done altogether. Or so I imagine, anyway.

The lounge was like most I'd been in in other Complexes, except that the furnishings were slightly more elegant and there weren't as many Servos, only three men with electric waste-disposals and two women with little hand-vacs for cleaning the lint off your clothing. The Fueltender was an Oriental, of course: The Union wouldn't take any other race these days, although Fueltending and a lot of other professions were supposed to be opening up at Luna Colony. He had an old-style Fu Manchu mustache and Fu Manchu fingernails painted a bright crimson and his hands were so quick and so deft handling the Fuel containers that it was like watching a TriDim magic act. His name was Ralph.

"How's it going, Ralph?" I said.

"Just fine, Mr. Sackett," Ralph said. "I was hoping you'd come in so I could tell you how much I admired your prose-making on TriDim today."

"Well, thanks."

"You'll go all the way now, I'm certain of it. It was a textbook performance."

I Fueled up. It hit me just right, like the petals of a rose slowly opening up in my stomach—little soft ripples of warmth. "You really think so?" I said.

"Oh, yes," Ralph said. "I don't know if I mentioned this before, but I've been studying your technique for some time. My ambition is to become a New-Sport professional myself someday."

I gave him a quizzical look. He hadn't told me that before and I found it sort of interesting. There had never been an Oriental pulpeteer as far as I knew, or a black or Chicano pulpeteer either. I wondered if that was because those races had something lacking in their genetic equipment, as maybe was (or maybe wasn't) the case with women, or if it was simply that young minority wordsmiths never had the opportunities to compete that young Caucasian wordsmiths did. Things were a lot better for blacks and Orientals and Chicanos nowadays than they had been in the twentieth century, but still, it made you wonder.

"I hope you make it, Ralph," I said. "If there's ever anything I can do, just let me know."

"I will, Mr. Sackett. But if I'm going to succeed, I want

to do it on my own." He shrugged and then said, as if changing the subject: "It was shameful, the way Harmon Penn treated you in the post-game interview. But there's a rumor circulating now that his popularity is on the wane and he'll eventually be replaced. Wouldn't it be fine if the rumor was true?"

"It sure would, Ralph," I said. "It sure would."

Another customer called to him for a reFuel and he moved away down the bar. Right away three of the Servos approached me and hovered around, looking for lint to vac away or something to dispose of. When I took out my pipe and tamped tobacco into it, another Servo came up to light a match; and as soon as I had the pipe drawing, he popped the burnt matchstick into his little electric cube and incinerated it.

There isn't much work for the Servos, so they have to keep busy the best ways they can. That's one of the unwritten rules among them, whether they work in lounges or any other aspect of society. Servos and society, I thought as I took a little more of my Fuel. The two went hand in hand, so to speak, and had for more than forty years, ever since the Reconstruction and the brilliant perceptions of the government of that era. If it hadn't been for the Servos, there probably wouldn't be any society left at all.

The fact was, after the Crash of 2006 there was almost no work for all but the most highly trained people. Functions, just as had been predicted in the Quality Lit of a century ago, had been pretty much passed onto machines, which could do them better and without the kind of resentments that had led to what were called "the social dislocations of the sixties and beyond." But the use of servomechanisms—computers, simulators, micros, household robos—had led to things even worse than the great dislocations. It had led to an enormous, sullen class of people, maybe 80 percent of the population on the Assistance Rolls; and it had led to a lot of social anarchy, personal and family breakdown, and so on because these people had nothing to *do*. The Reconstruction government had seen that the trend simply had to be reversed or matters would have become intolerable. They had to get the people back to work. The servomechanisms would keep order and make society functional, but people would have to have something to do too, something useful, no matter how minor, for their own self-image.

So the concept of Servos had been created. Every person on the Assistance Rolls had been required to choose what sort of necessary, if menial, Servo task he or she wanted to perform from an official government list advertised on TriDim and by Informationals. A special agency had been set up to oversee the program, with branch offices in each of the megalopolises and in the Rural Lands as well. This agency saw to it that each Servo was paid a standard wage, with cost-of-living increases and other benefits. They also ran periodic spot checks to make sure each Servo was tending to his duties, mediated in disputes, and prevented disruption of services arising from too many individuals wanting the same Servo position or territory.

And that was why one Fuel lounge in one Sky Complex had a minimum of five Servos when a single machine could have done the job; why every public aircab and groundcab had two pilots; why the lists of volunteer workers for the Luna Colony project were long and growing longer by the month. Most Servos were content in their jobs, though, because the work was easy and they made a decent living. Of course, there wasn't much incentive for them to better themselves. But then there wasn't much incentive for anybody, the structure of things being what it was. You just had to be content with what you had and what you were.

Unless what you were was a pulpeteer, and you were in a position to win the Prose Bowl.

That started me thinking about the second great perception of the Reconstruction government, which concerned the decline and near-collapse of universal literacy. The culture itself had been threatened: not reading when it was a matter of fiction or documentary was harmless enough, but not reading when it meant that even simple Informationals couldn't be understood was actively dangerous. It became apparent to the politicians that reading would have to be reinstituted, just as the jobless trend had to be reversed, by bold and unconventional means.

The only way to reinstitute reading, they decided, was to make writing itself a kind of sport—an ultimate sport that would appeal to the great and glamorous sport culture. They felt that the public could be led, through identification with pulpeteers who were competing publicly for prizes of considerable value, to accept at least a minimum literacy standard, if only so they could follow the prose being written by their favorite wordsmiths. So it was government aid that helped to found the New-Sport leagues, each one based on the categories of twentieth-century prose fiction (which was the last fiction ever to be written and published or taped); and government aid which helped to promote New-Sport with such a fervor that within a few decades it had not only eclipsed such Old-Sports as baseball and football in popularity, it had rendered them obsolete.

Before long a top pulpeteer had the status and the earning potential of any Old-Sport figure of the earlier generations, and it was pulpeteers who were doing all the endorsements, and holding the summer camps for kids, and appearing on TriDim variety shows. And as Old-Sport died out altogether, except for fanatical amateur leagues scattered here and there in the Rural Lands, the literacy standard had begun gradually to rise, just as predicted. Today it was almost to what it had been back in the 1980s.

Some said New-Sport and Servos were pretty shaky underpinnings for a culture as complicated, as crowded as ours. But I didn't agree with that at all. As far as I was concerned I and the rest of the prosemakers were doing nothing less than helping to provide humanity with a solid foundation for the future. Which was about as important and meaningful a task as anybody in the country was performing these days.

I sipped some more of my Fuel, enjoying it as I thought

about all of these historical and social facts, basking in the quiet, almost reverential attention of the Servos. From time to time I looked over at the entrance, waiting for Huxtable to appear, but mostly I didn't think about him. The Fuel had done its good work; I felt loose now, at peace—poised on the kind of fragile balance Fuel sometimes sets up inside you, the best feeling in the world when it happens.

Sally doesn't think so, of course. Now and again she'd complain to me about Fueling up. "Don't you see, Rex?" she'd say. "The peace and the good feelings have to come from inside you, not from the Fuel. The government and the Informational agencies are just trying to make you believe in lies when they tell you anything else; they control the Fuel supply, and if you feel your happiness is dependent on Fuel, then you're dependent on *them*. Don't you see that?"

Well, no, I didn't see it. And I didn't want to try, especially not now.

Huxtable finally appeared at nineteen fifteen hours. He was wearing a wing-collared tunic and jodhpurs in place of his Editor's garb, and he looked pretty suave; there was none of the air of authority about him that he seemed to have on the field. When he came over I gestured to Ralph and used my Unlimited card to buy him a container of Fuel. I was feeling generous, there was no doubt about that. The last thing I'd normally do was buy an Editor a drink.

"Must feel pretty good," he said.

"What must?"

"Having an Unlimited card."

"Sure," I said. "And it'll be good for life after I win the Bowl next week."

Huxtable took his Fuel from Ralph and drank some of it, waving Ralph away with his free hand. "You're sure you're going to win?" he said to me.

"Yes," I said, "I am."

"You really want to win, right?"

That seemed like a strange question from an Editor. In fact, it seemed strange just to be talking to an Editor off the field, much less drinking with one; Editors and prosemakers seem to have an uncomfortable relationship at the best of times. "Why do you ask that?" I said.

"I'm interested in you, kid."

"Why?"

"Because *next year* is yours and I'm always looking ahead."

"Next year?"

"If you're smart, that is. If you work together with people like me, people who'd like to see you protect your future."

I frowned, feeling confused. What was Huxtable trying to say? What sort of investment deal was he leading up to?

"I don't understand," I said.

"It's simple, kid. Next year is your year; next year you win the Prose Bowl."

"But I'm going to win it *this* year—"

"Uh-uh. This year you win something else."

"Like what?"

"Like five million dollars," Huxtable said.

"*What?*"

"Five million dollars. Double the championship prize: a major investment for your future. All yours, Sackett—in cash, no taxes to worry about."

My confusion was starting to give way to an uneasiness mingled with suspicion. "Why would you want to put that kind of money into my hands? Where would you get it?"

"It's not me who wants to put it into your hands," Huxtable said. "It's a certain group I represent, a group that's interested in the Prose Bowl outcome. I'm just a spokesman for them, see."

"What do they want me to do for that much money?"

"Nothing much. Just pull that hamstring of yours again along about the third quarter next Sunday."

"My hamstring?"

"Pull it real bad," Huxtable said. "So bad you can't continue with the match. So bad you have to withdraw."

I stared at him; the full impact of what he was suggesting

began to burst in on me through the thin haze from the Fuel. "If I withdraw, then I forfeit the Prose Bowl," I said. "That's the idea, isn't it? You want me to deliberately lose the match."

I guess my voice must have gotten louder, because Ralph and a couple of the patrons were looking at us. Huxtable's hand pressed my arm, not gently, and he said in an undertone, "Don't be a fool, kid. Keep your voice down, shut up." His fingers dug harder into my arm and his eyes stared at and through me, and for the first time I realized what a hard-boiled type he was, just like the hoods and gunsels in twentieth-century Suspense Fic.

"No," I said, but I kept my voice low. "No, I won't do it."

"Sure you will," he said. "You just need a chance to think about it. So sleep on it overnight; tomorrow morning you'll see it our way."

"Never. I've worked all my life to get to the Prose Bowl—"

"You're twenty-four years old, you don't know what life is. Now you take The Cranker. He's fifty-seven: *He's* worked all his life to get to the Prose Bowl and maybe he won't make it past Fast-Action Eddie tonight, maybe he won't get there at all. But suppose he does. Wouldn't it be kind of nice to have the old man win it?"

"Is The Cranker involved in this too? Is that it?"

"He's no more involved than you," Huxtable said. "Pulpeteers don't matter here; this is something a lot bigger than you or any other prose hack. So what do you say? Are you going to do it without a fuss?"

"No," I said.

"Tomorrow morning the answer better be yes."

I slammed my Fuel container down and got to my feet. Ralph looked at me with concern and so did a couple of the Servos, but I just shook my head at them. There was no point in starting an incident, not in here; Huxtable might be armed, for one thing, and there might even be other members of his group lurking nearby.

"I'm leaving," I said. "And you'd better not bother me again."

Out of the side of his mouth Huxtable repeated, "Tomorrow morning, and the answer better be yes," as I turned away from him. "If it isn't, Sackett, you're going to regret it real bad."

I put my back to him and walked out of the lounge. And it wasn't until I was in the chute that the full significance of what had happened in there struck me with delayed force and started my knees shaking. An attempt to fix the Prose Bowl! What amounted to a threat on my life! It was outrageous, it was incredible, it was—

And then I had an odd and terrible thought.

What if it had happened to other Prose Bowl finalists before me?

5

By the time I reached my apartment the effects of the Fuel had already begun to fade; tension and anger and a sense of helplessness had replaced the feelings of looseness and peace. I security-locked the door and went straight to the vicom, switching on both audio and visual as I dialed Mort's home number.

His image and voice came on seconds later. He wasn't alone; but the person he was with was Diana Pollard, his red-haired secretary and girlfriend, so I knew it was all right to talk. She knows the business almost as well as Mort does.

"You look shaky, Rex," he said. "What's the matter?"

"Somebody wants me to throw the Prose Bowl," I said grimly.

Mort's eyes widened. "Say that again."

"An Assistant Line Editor named Huxtable—you know who he is, I think—he offered me five million dollars to fake another hamstring pull and then withdraw."

There was a pause while Mort digested all of that. In the background I could hear noises from the building under construction next to Mort's; Diana kept glancing toward the windows, as if she wished she could go over there and cut off the electricity on all of their power tools.

"When did all this happen?" Mort said finally. "What did you do?"

"It happened in the lounge right here in my Complex, just now. I told him I wasn't going to do it."

"Did you call anybody else before me?"

"No."

"Good. Okay, you did the right thing with Huxtable. Now you've got to put the whole episode out of your mind."

"Put it out of my mind?"

"Yes," Mort said. "You turned the proposal down, that's the main thing. Huxtable won't be editing in the Prose Bowl; there's nothing he can do."

"But Mort—"

"Listen to me, now." His voice was confident, trust-inspiring as always. "This all ties in with the resurgence of gambling at Luna Colony; the lid is off up there, you know that."

Well, I did know it. There had been a TriDim documentary on Luna Colony just last week. It was something like Alaska had been a century and a half ago, or the Malay Archipelago in the late 1990s: a territory just opening up to construction and civilization, mainly populated by the sort of people Mom likes to call "lowlifes" from America, China, Russo-Europe, and other areas. There are murders on Luna all the time, and other crimes of brutality—one of the reasons, according to the TriDim documentary, being that the colony is mostly building up underground and there's a lot of psychological stress in subterranean living. And even though comparatively few women live there, there's some sinning of flesh too. But it's gambling that's the most prevalent of all the vices. There's something about new territories that brings out the wagering instinct in men, the TriDim narrator had said, and he was probably right. It's in the blood, I guess.

"They bet on the size of the surface craters, anything to keep themselves amused," Mort was saying. "It's not surprising that some of them would get together, find a stooge like Huxtable, and try to fix the Prose Bowl; it's the lure of major competition. It doesn't mean a thing, though."

"But isn't it *serious?* I mean, shouldn't we report it to the authorities?"

"Absolutely not," Mort said. "Huxtable would only deny it and it'd be your word against his. And worst of all, somebody like Penn would get hold of the story and have a field day on TriDim, insinuating all sorts of things. The last thing we need is that kind of publicity, kid. What kind of shape do you think you'd be in by the time the Big Face-Off rolls around on Sunday?" He paused to study the image of my face. "No," he said, "you just sit tight. If anything else happens, let me know right away. But I don't think anything will. They tried, they failed, that's the end of it. Okay?"

"I don't know, Mort," I said. "I still think—"

"Don't think," he said. "That's what you pay me forty-five percent for. Just forget it. And try to relax. Watch the West Coast semifinal on TriDim, then go to bed and get a good night's sleep. Talk to you tomorrow."

He disconnected, and the sudden disappearance of his image was somehow a little unsettling. It seemed unfair of him not to talk this over with me at greater length. And yet, on the other hand, his advice made sense. I *had* to trust his judgment; he had brought me this far, hadn't he?

I went to the window and looked out over the mega-lopolis again, thinking about Mort and a lot of other things. Somehow the uneasy feelings would not go away. And the hazy lights of New York did nothing to cheer me up, as they sometimes did; the garish reds and greens and purples of the Informationals, most of them advertising the New-Sport play-offs and now the upcoming Prose Bowl, along with holiday items and such products as Quasi-Fuel and Quasi-Smokes, seemed to make a less cheerful blaze of color against the cold night sky than usual. In fact, they looked somehow tawdry, false, like one of the background scenes in a TriDim "Twentieth-Century Playhouse" production.

I paced around for a while, aimlessly looking at the prose posters—mockups of what used to be called dust jackets—decorating my walls. All the greats were there, the giants of those bygone years: *Pale Fire, The Space Merchants, Mansion of Deadly Desire, Smoking Guns of the Barricade Bunch, The Running of Beasts, Nurse Conrad Sees It Through, The Grapes of Wrath, The Transvection Machine, Hour of the Oxrun*

Dead, The Maltese Falcon. But they didn't do anything to
cheer me up either. About the only thing that would, I decided, was another small container of Fuel and the TriDim
cast of the Culp-Duke Face-Off out in Las Vegas. At least in
another few hours I'd know who my opponent would be in the
Prose Bowl; then I could start focusing my thoughts on strategy and a game plan that I could discuss later with Mort.

I opened a mini-container and then switched on the Tri-
Dim and settled back in front of the screen, letting the sounds
and the movement wrap themselves around me. The first image to appear, though, was of none other than Harmon Penn—
one-quarter life-size, brandishing a microphone and screaming
into it. He gets around, all right, I thought bitterly. Taunting
me in the New York Ultradome in the morning; then out to
Las Vegas by superjet to taunt the other semifinal winner in
the evening. There was something inescapable about the man.
I told myself I shouldn't resent him as much as I did, that he
was only trying to do a job, just like all of us were; but it
wasn't a very convincing argument. His job, at least as he
practiced it, depended on making people miserable, so why
shouldn't I resent the fat little bastard?

The other announcer was one I didn't know well, Lloyd
Sheldrake, who was a network swing man based on the West
Coast. He seemed knowledgeable enough: He was an ex-
pulpeteer who had played in the Horse Opera League many
years ago. He and Penn did some pre-game warm-up commentary and ran taped interviews with Fast-Action Eddie and
The Cranker. Culp looked kind of shaky in the close-ups—an
old man with hollows in his cheeks and strange peering eyes;
but his voice was level and there was something about him
that told me the age, the lines were mainly a kind of mask. He
gave Penn absolutely nothing on the tape; I had to envy the
way he handled him. "I have no comment on that," he said
time and again, and nothing Penn tried stirred him enough to
make him say anything he didn't want to say. There were
things I could learn from Leon Culp, there was no doubt
about that.

Fast-Action Eddie, who was thirty-two years old (although some of us felt he lied about his age, took three or four years off the way some did when they moved into the Bigs), was interviewed by Sheldrake and didn't quite show the same style as The Cranker. Still, he knew what he was doing too. "Leon Culp is one of the greats," he said, "one of the absolute greats, and it's an honor to face-off against him. Win or lose, I consider it a victory just to compete with his caliber of pro." But there was a certain expression in his eyes—humor or disdain, perhaps—which showed that he didn't mean what he said as sincerely as he seemed to. That maybe he felt The Cranker was over the hill and the best way to exploit his advantages of youth and quick wit was to humor the old lion. It wouldn't work, I thought, not with Culp. But it wouldn't hurt either and showed a kind of ingratiating humility. There were things I could learn from Fast-Action Eddie, too.

Both The Cranker and Duke were asked about me, of course, and I had to admire how they handled that as well. Culp said he assumed I was a good pulpeteer—twenty-four and in the Prose Bowl spoke for itself. Fast-Action Eddie said I reminded him a little of himself at twenty-four, talented but perhaps a little inexperienced. I felt myself empathizing with both of them in different ways, although with The Cranker there was a little awe and hero worship mixed in too.

After the interviews a series of Informationals came on, one of which had some good new singing and dancing for one of the Quasi-Fuel brands. Then Sheldrake and Penn talked for a while about the upcoming match and about my face-off this morning against the Kansas City Flash, obviously filling time. Sheldrake pointed out that regardless of tonight's outcome, the Prose Bowl would feature two first-timers, something which hadn't happened in five years. Penn said a little sourly that the primary reason for this was Wally Gold's tragic Luna accident: Wee-Wristed Wally had just hit his stride last year and would no doubt have scuffed the likes of Fast-Action Eddie, The Cranker, and The Metaphor Kid on his way to building a New-Sport dynasty. I didn't like that very much. And

Sheldrake, probably thinking of the ratings to come for the Prose Bowl, said that he disagreed, that The Cranker was one of the immortals, if maybe slightly past his prime, and Fast-Action Eddie was one of the top five journeymen in New-Sport, and I was the best young pulpeteer to come into the professional ranks in the last decade. Penn just shrugged and smiled in his smug superior way. The thing you had to keep reminding yourself about him was that he didn't like anything or anybody, maybe not even himself.

There were more Informationals, and when the stadium reappeared on the screen the lights had been dimmed for the playing of the National Anthem. Then, after some fast panning shots of the two booster sections and some close-ups of The Cranker and Fast-Action Eddie waiting at the Line, the Head Editor came trotting out for the coin flip. I found myself leaning into the holography with a good deal of anticipation. New-Sport gets into you with all its pageantry and excitement. It really does. At heart, I guess all of us are fans.

Culp won the coin toss; when the plot topics selected by the officials flashed on the scoreboards he took the toughest of the two, PLOTLESS QUALITY LIT, which was typical of the old warhorse. Fast-Action Eddie got OLD-SPORT—TEAM GAME.

Then the opening claxon sounded and the match was on.

6

The Cranker jumped out to an early lead, the way he almost always did in his face-offs; he wrote the first two hundred words in a single blinding burst of speed, slacked off just slightly for seventy-five or so, and then used a brilliant stream-of-consciousness Quality Lit technique to lay out another four hundred straight. Fast-Action Eddie's forte was what had given him his nickname: fast-paced, hard-driving narrative prose. Nobody could top him at that; it was why he had won the Suspense Fic championship three years in a row. But narrative hooks and transition gave him a little trouble and so he was a notoriously slow starter, even when he had a plot topic he could run with like Old-Sport—Team Game.

By the midway point in the first period, Culp had built up a 178-word lead; the scoreboard, which the TriDim cameras panned to constantly so the viewers could watch each pro's printout roll out as it was written, read: CULP 1004, DUKE 826.

I paid close attention to The Cranker on each of the close-ups, watching his face and the blurred movement of his fine old hands, the way I always did when he was in competition on TriDim. He was a classic study: the tilt of his head, those marvelous hands, the jaunty angle at which his cigarette, spiraling smoke, jutted from one corner of his mouth. His concentration was absolute; his eyes didn't blink once and not a muscle quivered anywhere in his seamed face.

He was at the top of his talent tonight too, you could tell that by the early quality and savage intensity of his prose. One passage in particular made me gasp with its incandescence:

REELING, THE DARKNESS SPINNING, THE SPIN-NING RIM OF DARKNESS MOVING EVER FASTER, DRIVING HIM INWARD, INWARD TOWARD THAT SMALL HARD PLACE OF IMPACT WHERE THERE WERE NO QUESTIONS, NO ANSWERS, BUT ONLY CIR-CUMSTANCE KNOWN OVER AND AGAIN, THE THIN COLD STONE OF CIRCUMSTANCE. REELING IN THE DARKNESS, HE THOUGHT OF THE CIRCUMSTANCE OF STONE, THAT GREAT AND TERRIBLE INTERFACE BETWEEN THE SPRINGING LIGHT OF ALL BEGIN-NING, AND OF THE COLD STROKING INARTICULATE DARKNESS WHERE AT LAST STONE AND LIFE TO-GETHER DEPARTED DUMB IN THE WHISPERS OF FISHES, CRAWLING THINGS, LOST THINGS, UN-KNOWN THINGS: AT LAST, AT LAST THE SEA.

The TriDim technicians split the screen so that they could run the instant replay on the one side while the match continued on the other. They slowed it to three-quarter speed, letting you see each phrase come out slowly, and then they flipped it back again and ran it at double-speed so that the phrase appeared with terrific force. At both speeds The Cranker's brilliance only became more evident. Sometimes the replays expose flaws in technique, point up weaknesses or hesitations which in the heat of battle go undetected, but I couldn't see any weaknesses at all. Even Penn was awed, or maybe just silent because even he couldn't think of anything negative to say.

I shook my head in wonder. There was no way you could beat The Cranker when he was on top of his game; all you could hope for was that he'd fail to sustain his levels when he got tired. That was what had happened to him in his three previous play-off appearances. But I had a feeling, watching him now, that this time it would be a different story: that at last, at the age of fifty-seven, his time had come and he was going to make it all the way through to the Prose Bowl.

Fast-Action Eddie wasn't conceding anything yet, though. Down by as much as two hundred words at one point, he had overcome his characteristic slow start and was beginning to pound with a stubborn and deadly ferocity.

"PUCK!" HE HEARD EVANS, THE GOALIE SHRIEK. "I LOST THE PUCK!" AND IMMEDIATELY THE RABBIT SPUN LOOSE BEHIND THE NET, HIS BLUE JERSEY SOAKED WITH SWEAT, SEARCHING FOR THE SMALL RUBBER DISK AS THE RED PLAYERS CONVERGED AHEAD OF HIM. KEEP DRIVING, HE TOLD HIMSELF AS HE DARTED INTO THE MIDST OF THE REDS, DODGING THE MASSIVE RED CENTER'S INSOLENTLY FLICKING STICK. FIND THE PUCK. GET THE PUCK OUT OF HERE.

"Duke, Duke, Duke!" his boosters were screaming. *"Puke, puke, puke! Ed-die Duke! King of puke!"*

"Fast-Action Eddie's making his move now, folks," Lloyd Sheldrake was saying. He always got excited during his word-by-word account of a face-off; the faster a pulpeteer punched out his prose, the faster Sheldrake talked. "He may have been slow out of the starting gate tonight but he's making up for lost time now, he's really grinding out the old pulp. Only a hundred and seventy-five words down now; the match is tightening up, even though The Cranker is still firing some of the most dazzling Quality Lit prose these old eyes have ever seen. Take that line a couple of minutes ago: 'stone and life together departed dumb in the whispers of fishes'—boy, that's really one of your all-time originals—"

"On the contrary," Penn's stagily sepulchral voice interrupted, "Culp used a similar line in the quarterfinals back in Forty-five."

"He did? Are you sure about that, Harmon?"

"Of course I'm sure," Penn snapped. "Are you questioning me? Don't ever question me. The line was: 'bones and

strife together departing numb in the whispers of ancient pha-
raohs.' You can look it up; our viewers can look it up. The
Cranker may not be a has-been, as some of our more percep-
tive scribes have been saying, but he certainly does seem to be
repeating quite a few of his past successes . . ."

It was getting so I hated the sound of his voice. I shut it
out with a conscious effort, concentrating even harder on the
images of Culp and Duke and the prose they were making
under the glaring stadium lights.

THE RABBIT LET FLY WITH A SAVAGERY THAT
BELIED HIS NICKNAME, SLAP-SHOOTING FROM THE
CENTER LINE. THE PUCK WINGED PAST MORRIS,
CAROMED OFF DEVEREAUX'S STICK, AND ELUDED
THE DESPERATE GRAB OF THE RED GOALIE. SCORE!
THE BLUES HAD TAKEN THE LEAD . . . BUT WAIT,
NOW A FIGHT WAS STARTING, STICKS WERE FLYING.
THE RABBIT FORGOT HIS EXCITEMENT OVER HIS
GOAL, BARED HIS TOOTHLESS GUMS, AND KNOCKED
THE RED GOALIE INTO THE NET ON TOP OF THE
PUCK.

"Action, Action—Fast, Fast, Fast!"

IT WAS THE PAIN, THE ANGUISH, THE QUINTES-
SENCE OF MISERY AND SELF-LOATHING THAT HE
SOUGHT WITHIN THE GREAT AND WRITHING SWEL-
TER WHICH TIGHTENED AROUND HIM, FEELING IN
THAT FIRST GREAT ECLIPSE OF THE ENCLOSURE
THE SLOW DEADENING BEGINNING AT THE ROOT,
THEN MOVING THROUGH ALL THE TENDRILS INTO
THE AQUEOUS MEDIUM OF HIS HERITAGE, THE RIP-
PLES DARKENING YET SOOTHING, LIKE THE MOVE-
MENT OF THE RUINED SEA AND THE RUINED
BLOOD.

"Culp, Culp, churn that pulp!"

The Cranker churned through to the two-thousand-word
mark on his next sentence, ending the first quarter; the machines locked with the scoreboard reading: CULP 2000,
DUKE 1856.

Standing, holding his Fuel container raised to the crowd, Fast-Action Eddie seemed determined to wait out the quarter break without resting. But The Cranker sat limply at his typewriter while his Servos moved cold towels over his face and lit fresh cigarettes for him. His lips were moving; on the close-ups I could see him mouthing the words of his final sentence, as if preparing himself for the sentences and paragraphs to follow.

Sheldrake and Penn chattered through the two-minute time-out, comparing the performances of Culp and Fast-Action Eddie with those of previous matches, wondering if the random categories they'd been given were any factor. Penn thought they were. "It's possible, you know, to pad Quality Lit to a degree impossible in the tighter and more formularized Old-Sports field," he said, and Sheldrake said politely, "Well, Harmon, it seems to me that padding is possible in all the categories with equal ease." Penn knew absolutely nothing about pulpeteers or prosemaking, but Sheldrake wasn't much better; like many failed wordsmiths, he showed disdain for what was going on and seemed unaware of the true brilliance of what The Cranker had created so far. He even agreed when Penn said that the skill of a pulpeteer wasn't in his ability to work in any prose category, wasn't in padding or pacing or any of those technical things, but simply in the fact that he had plenty of time to study and practice because that was all he knew how to do. "In point of fact," the bastard said, "a pulpeteer is little more than a glorified Servo."

Then, mercifully, it was time for the second quarter to begin. The Cranker didn't stand up and go to the Line until the last possible second; and when he did, with the perpetual cigarette cocked in one corner of his mouth, he didn't glance once at Fast-Action Eddie. It was as if Fast-Action Eddie weren't even there; as if The Cranker were alone in the great stadium, performing not so much for the amusement of the seventy thousand fans as for the amusement of Leon Culp.

When the claxon sounded and the two of them were once more behind their machines, The Cranker attacked with the same brilliance and speed as in the opening period. More stream-of-consciousness, an array of adjectives, portmanteau words, obscure synonyms and antonyms, an offhand but sparklingly inventive double entendre that involved twenty-nine lines and had the crowd on its feet and even Penn making grudgingly impressed noises. Inside of ten minutes he had outscored Eddie Duke 1178 to 981 and taken a commanding 350-word lead. If he kept up this pace, he would be ahead by five hundred at the half and well on his way to a thousand-word scuff.

But he didn't keep up his pace, not quite. He seemed to settle into a kind of holding pattern—a comfortable groove in which he was content to maintain that 350-word margin while pursuing an even higher quality prose. Maybe he was saving himself for the second half, the grueling final stretch run; maybe he was just toying with Fast-Action Eddie. It didn't matter. All that mattered was that he was on, he was magnificent, and it was almost as exciting watching him tonight as it had been for me that first time against Three-Finger Luke Waddell those many years ago.

SPLITTING THE EDGES OF HIS FEELING, THEN, HE COULD FEEL THAT BISECTION AS SOMEHOW SYMBOLIC OF THE SCHISM WITH WHICH HE HAD LIVED ALL OF HIS LIFE: ON THE LEFT ALL THAT HE HAD WANTED TO BE, HAD BELIEVED IN, HAD SEEN IN THE SANCTIMONIOUS AND DARK SPACES OF YOUTH, ON THE RIGHT THE SMALLER AND LESS PRECISE RESONANCES OF WHAT HE HAD BECOME, ODORS OF FAILURE, STINK OF DEFEAT, WHISK OF DARKNESS, ROTTEN CORE OF CULPABILITY . . . OH YES, HE COULD SEE IT NOW AND WHAT MATTERED MORE THAN ANYTHING WAS THAT IT WAS GOOD. HE COULD BEAR HIMSELF NOW. HE KNEW NOT ONLY WHAT HE HAD BEEN BUT WHAT HE MUST BECOME AND THE THOUGHT HORRIFIED

The Line Editor's claxon blared.

Halftime.

The Cranker's machine had locked at four thousand on the word HORRIFIED; Fast-Action Eddie, at 3641, was trailing by almost the same margin that had existed since early in the second quarter. But from the look on Duke's face as he stood slowly, as he reached with clutching hand for the Fuel container one of his Servos extended, he felt the deficit was much greater than that: that it was insurmountable.

Culp gave no sign of knowing this or of what he might be feeling. He took a Fuel container from his own Servos, waved them away, and sat staring up at the transparent plastoid dome. If he had had any trouble with too much Fuel in the past, it seemed well behind him; he drank it now as meditatively and calmly as if he had been a minister doing a religious Informational. I felt the awe and reverence moving through me again as I looked at him and it was only as the cameras tracked away, first focusing on Penn and Sheldrake in the booth, then spinning into a long series of crowd and band shots, that I realized that I had allowed myself to become intimidated.

It shouldn't have happened, I should have guarded against it; and yet, the old man had been really magnificent. I decided I could use some Fuel myself and started to get up. But then I thought that if I couldn't face the power of The Cranker without Fuel as a TriDim viewer, how could I possibly do so as his competitor? I sank back down again, warning myself to think positively. What was happening to Fast-Action Eddie Duke was *not* going to happen to The Metaphor Kid.

There was a series of Informationals and then Penn and Sheldrake came back on. Penn's attitude had shifted somewhat during the break; now he seemed to be on The Cranker's side. That's one thing about Penn: He doesn't like to be identified with a losing position and won't stay with one once he realizes that's what it is.

"One must admit that Culp certainly has put it all together out there tonight," he said, "in spite of his tendency to repeat himself. There is a drive and energy and snap to his

prose that we haven't seen for many years; this is the legend-
ary Leon Culp reborn."

"A very impressive performance, all right," Sheldrake
agreed. "And he's done it on a moderate Fuel consumption,
too."

The cameras tracked Fast-Action Eddie coming back
from his locker room for the second half. He looked worried
and maybe still a little dazed; his eyes had a faraway glaze
which I'd seen before in pros who were in danger of losing and
losing badly. The Cranker, on the other hand, looked both
implacable and serene—a pose that I knew well from watching him over the years, that could have a deadly effect on the
flagging morale of an opponent.

"It looks to me," Penn said, "as though Duke has lost
some of his competitive edge. I think Fast-Action Eddie will
become Slow-Action Eddie in the second half and it will be
The Cranker and the young upstart, Rex Sackett, in next Sunday's Prose Bowl."

Once the third quarter began there was no doubt in anybody's mind, least of all mine, that Penn was right. The
Cranker came out at top speed again, working now like a man
thirty years younger, a man my own age, with fire in his fingers as well as on the board, and the range of the work itself
was dazzling; he was piling up savage and multilined metaphors, working intricate little variations on the pathetic fal-
lacy of prose—that outside conditions symbolize character
moods, and vice versa—which had never before been seen in
competition outside the Quality Lit League.

Fast-Action Eddie was still game; you had to give him
that. There was one pretty moment in the middle of the quarter that made it clear to me, if not to Penn, that he was a true
top-line pro whose three straight Suspense Fic crowns had
been no fluke.

THE PUCK SLAMMED SWAYING INTO THE NET,
SLIDING BACK AND FORTH RHYTHMICALLY, THEN
COMING TO REST. GOAL! THE RABBIT FELT AS HE
SKATED BY THAT THE PUCK WAS WINKING AT HIM.

THAT WAS HOW IT GOT SOMETIMES IN THE ACTION
OF A TOUGH CONTEST: A SPECIAL COMMUNICATION
DEVELOPED BETWEEN HIMSELF AND THE PUCK,
JUST THE PUCK AND THE RABBIT TALKING TO EACH
OTHER ACROSS CENTER ICE.

THE BLUES WERE PANTING AROUND HIM AT
THE FACE-OFF, THEIR EYES TURNED TO HIM IN AP-
PEAL. IT'S UP TO YOU, RABBIT, THOSE EYES WERE
SAYING, IT'S ALL UP TO YOU. THEN THE PUCK
DROPPED AND HIS STICK WAS OUT LIKE A TONGUE
LASHING AT IT; HE HIT THE PUCK HARD AND FOR
AN INSTANT IT SEEMED TO BE HEADING TOWARD
THE RED'S OPEN GOAL MOUTH. THEN AT THE LAST
MOMENT IT WAS FLICKED ASIDE AND HE HEARD
THE OFFICIAL'S WHISTLE BLOW. ICING. AND ICE
SPREAD THROUGH HIS HEART.

"Great stuff," Sheldrake said as the instant replay came
on. "Just great. Major league."

"Too little," Penn said portentously, "and too late."

"Still—"

"The horse is gone and the stable door is locked," Penn
said.

The Cranker's margin was 530 words now and he was
closing in on the third-quarter mark. Muted cheers from the
crowd spilled out around me, but even Culp's booster section
seemed as awed as the rest of us; there is something about true
greatness demonstrated publicly that's humbling. He closed a
loop on a foreshadowing from back in the second quarter and
then, to end the third period with a flourish, he punched out a
stunning surprise reversal of form which had Penn muttering
laudatory comparisons to a twentieth-century pro named John
Cheever.

CULP 6000, DUKE 5449.

I couldn't watch when the cameras homed in on Fast-
Action Eddie's face; he looked stricken, lost, with some of that
same inexplicable, hollowed-out sense of personal tragedy that
I'd seen in the Kansas City Flash's face this afternoon. He was

finished and he knew it. And he was having trouble coping with the fact inside his own mind.

The beginning of the final two-thousand-word block was just like all the others: The Cranker whipped out a fast five hundred words before Fast-Action Eddie could even get back into the flow of his prose. But Culp was tiring a little now; you could see that. Penn and Sheldrake could see it too and began commenting on it, but not in a negative way. Penn didn't even make one of his usual nasty remarks when The Cranker, to almost everyone's surprise, took a nonchalant twenty-second Fuel penalty with the score at 7009 to 6166. Culp could afford the luxury and he knew it just as well as Fast-Action Eddie knew he was beaten.

The last thousand words of The Cranker's scuff seemed as if they would go by at a leisurely pace; it took almost fifteen minutes for him to ease out six hundred of them. But in that same amount of time Duke only scored four hundred and eighty, and all of those weak and of near-penalty carelessness. The final margin, I thought, was going to be around twelve hundred words.

Only it didn't work out quite that way. With the score at 7713 to 6689, Fast-Action Eddie stood up abruptly and took a twenty-second Fuel penalty of his own. Then, after swallowing at least six ounces, he set the container down on the turf beside his chair and respectfully saluted The Cranker.

I leaned forward in the same astonishment that everybody watching must have felt. Even Penn and Sheldrake were quiet. The cameras came in tight on Fast-Action Eddie's face—and, even more amazingly, he began to type words that his printout told us had nothing to do with Old-Sport—Team Game.

YOU'RE TOO GOOD TONIGHT, CRANKER. TO-NIGHT YOU'RE THE BEST THERE EVER WAS AND WE ALL KNOW IT. I CAN'T BEAT YOU.

The Cranker was peering at the scoreboard facing him, his expression set oddly. He didn't seem to know how to react. Or maybe he just wasn't able to react.

Fast-Action Eddie saluted again. I CONCEDE THE MATCH, his printout said. YOU'RE THE WINNER, JUST AS YOU DESERVE TO BE. MY BEST WISHES IN THE PROSE BOWL.

And then Fast-Action Eddie Duke stood up again, waved to the crowd, and with his head held erect he walked the long walk to the sidelines and tunnel beyond.

I sat there in the silence that seemed to swell in the room around me, in the sudden thunder that followed moments later and reached an almost deafening pitch. Penn's voice, barely audible, was saying as the cameras alternated between the retreating figure of Fast-Action Eddie and Culp's seamed and serene form sitting motionless behind his machine, "Unprecedented, that's what it is. A direct typed resignation in the semifinals is absolutely without precedent in the history of New-Sport."

"You're forgetting Twenty-one, Harmon," Sheldrake said mildly. "Remember Limber Larry Lucchesi, who—"

Penn cut him off. I could imagine the furious expression on the fat little man's face when he said threateningly, "Don't you disagree with me. I am never wrong in my facts."

"I didn't mean to —"

"Don't you *ever* disagree with me," Penn said.

Fast-Action Eddie disappeared and the cameras stayed locked on Culp as the Head Editor waved his star-spangled Prose Bowl flag to declare the Face-Off ended; the P.A. announcer's voice boomed the final score and explained the concession under Rule 87, Paragraph 9 of the New-Sport Official Rule Manual. It was only after several minutes, it seemed, that an almost imperceptible smile, a weary and somehow pained smile, came over The Cranker's craggy features. Then his Servos arrived, and he took Fuel, and the smile widened, and when the announcer said that Leon Culp would be The Metaphor Kid's opponent in the Prose Bowl, The Cranker threw back his great head and laughed up at the dome and the dark sky.

It gave me a chill to see him do that, to watch this marvelous old pulpeteer standing there in glory tonight and know that he would be sitting across the Line from me next Sunday in Greater Los Angeles. How could I beat a legend like him? Could I even keep from being humiliated the way Fast-Action Eddie had?

I got quickly to my feet and shut off the TriDim; I felt drained, a little numb. It had been the longest and most exhausting day of my life, full of all sorts of highs and lows: the semifinal victory over Ollie Garbowitz, the interview with Penn, the party afterward, the odd way Sally had seemed to challenge me and my life-style, the bribe offer by Huxtable, Mort's reaction to the bribe offer, and then that unparalleled performance by The Cranker and my own doubts and worries about the Prose Bowl. It was a kind of overload: I couldn't handle any more input without short-circuiting somewhere.

I disconnected the vi-com before Mort or Sally or anybody else could call, and I went straight to bed and straight into a restless and nightmare-ridden sleep.

7

Snow was falling when I woke up on Monday morning—a dull silver curtain half-obscuring the winking blaze of the Informationals, the pattern of lights in the Sky Complexes. I felt stiff and cold and achey; the pulled hamstring in my right leg was so tight I couldn't walk without limping. For the first time in my life I had intimations of what it was like to be as old as The Cranker. What it was like to be *old*.

Most of the confusion of the night before was gone, but there were remnants of it clinging like cobwebs to the corners of my mind. The remnants of my nightmares clung there too, most of which were too flimsy to let me remember what they were about. But in one of them I seemed to be in an unfamiliar stadium, up on one of the scoreboards with somebody's prose printout appearing in foot-high letters across my chest; and in another my fingers and toes were typewriter keys that The Cranker was flailing at with his fantastic hands. I could also hear the ghostlike echoes of voices: Sally's, Mort's, Huxtable's saying over and over, "Tomorrow morning, and the answer better be yes. If it isn't, you're going to regret it real bad."

I poured myself a couple of ounces of Fuel, the first of the day. They went down easy and the slow unfolding began in my stomach, soothing me, warming me. I've always thought of that first sip of Fuel as being a narrative hook, a sort of opening premise that sets up a body of Fuel each day; and the last drink at night, of course, is the climax. I don't know if other pulpeteers tend to think of Fuel in this way, but maybe they do; in any event I told this once to Mort, who laughed and said, "The opening hook is all right, kid, but you'd better watch out for those delayed revelations."

I dialed and drank a vita-breakfast from the apartment's Nutritional Unit, then got into my training uniform and took the chute down to the rec room in the Complex's sub-basement. A half hour of running on the Exerciser belts loosened up my leg muscles; and another thirty minutes in the Body-Ease relaxed me and smoothed out my thoughts. I was almost feeling my old self again by the time I got back inside my apartment: ready to face not only the day but anything the day might bring.

Ready to face The Cranker too, I thought. So what if he was a legend? So what if his performance last night was the finest ever given in the Prose Bowl play-offs? I could still beat him next week: Next week it was a whole different match, and maybe he wouldn't have what he'd had against Fast-Action Eddie Duke. He was only a man, only a pulpeteer—and *he* had never been in the Prose Bowl either, let alone claimed the championship prize.

I could beat him, all right. And I would. This week may have belonged to The Cranker, but next week would belong to The Metaphor Kid.

I was smiling a little, feeling the old confidence building up solid inside me again, as I switched on the TriDim to catch the morning newscast. Culp's victory was headline news, as I'd expected it would be, but it didn't bother me now to watch his slashing prose attack on the taped replays. It didn't bother me, either, to listen to The Cranker discuss his triumph on a tape of the post-game interview. He seemed kind of subdued for a prosemaker who had just double-scuffed his opponent in such meteoric fashion; he didn't say much, answering most of the questions with monosyllables, and he seemed to be hitting the Fuel pretty hard. Maybe he was celebrating, but it looked more like he was using it to shore himself up, as if his performance had taken far more out of him than he wanted to let on.

About all he said of me was that he expected Rex Sackett to be a tough opponent; and all he said of the Prose Bowl was that yes, he was pleased and relieved to have made it to the championship round after all these years. The New-Sport announcer, once the tapes were over, praised Culp's effort against Fast-Action Eddie but was as cautious about predicting a Prose Bowl win for The Cranker as Culp himself had been. He called me an up-and-comer, with solid talent and surprising versatility for my age, and intimated that at this point he figured the Face-Off next Sunday to be a toss-up.

That cheered me even more. When I shut off the TriDim I remembered that I'd disconnected the vi-com last night; I switched it back on and decided I'd call Mort and see what he had to say about The Cranker's victory. But he didn't answer at his home or at his office, which probably meant that he was in transit from one to the other. Or maybe out for an early meeting with another of his clients.

I tried Sally's number then and she came on both audio and visual after fifteen seconds. She looked and sounded preoccupied, though, and didn't want to talk because she had an appointment at the Concertium at eleven and was just about to leave. There was a special retrospective concert today, Ravel or somebody, so she had to be there early to set up the music and stands for the musicians. That's one of the things she does as a Musicological Researcher and Recoverer, and if that isn't Servo work, I don't know what is.

She did say she'd be home around two if I wanted to stop by. I said I'd probably do that. After we switched off I thought about trying the folks, but Dad would be at his office by now and Mom did volunteer work on Mondays at the Informational Executives Retirement Home. So I tried Mort one more time instead. Still no answer.

Well, I knew he'd be in his offices later and I decided I'd go there and see him in person. I felt like getting out of the apartment and out of the Complex anyway: walking down on the streets—they were safe enough in the daytime, if you were careful and carried a tranq weapon in plain view—and breathing some nonfiltered air for a change, even though it was still spotted with contaminatives from the pre-Crash era of unrestricted industrial technology. I liked walking in the snow anyway. And if I stayed around here, I'd only be deluged with calls and visits from scribes, asking what I thought of The Cranker's victory. If I managed to avoid them until tonight, they'd probably lose interest again and leave me alone until something happened to stir them up another time.

I took a second small ration of Fuel and then rode the chute down to street level. Ordinarily I try not to Fuel up too much in the mornings. This is one of the first things a pulpeteer learns if he wants to stay around for a while; but then, as you grow up you understand that it's the exceptions that make life possible because life itself is an exception. The natural condition of circumstances is death, I wrote in the Historical Adventure League once, and although it cost me an orange-and-lilac penalty flag for Unjustified Generic Shift, I think it's a true line and one of my most profound.

I passed through the Checkpoint, nodding to the Servos on duty there, and walked outside. The snow was falling thick and damp in huge flakes that faded from white to dark as they settled; the air was heavy with weather smells, as the filtered indoors air isn't, and I found it exhilarating.

Walking is something that most people don't seem to enjoy nowadays, but I've never minded it. In my teens it was the time when I'd dream up some of my best plots and phrases and practice describing different weather conditions for those occasions in competition when I needed to fill up space and couldn't figure what the characters were supposed to be doing or how they were feeling. Weather is fairly easy to write, almost as easy for me as dialogue, which I've always had a knack for. Now, nostalgically, I breathed the cold air and watched the settling snowflakes and made notes to myself as to how I might work in snow if I drew Blazing Western Action again next Sunday, or Suspense Fic, or Quality Lit, or any of the other categories. Snow falling on horses was an interesting image, particularly since I had never seen a horse except in old photographs. I wondered how it would look.

The streets, as usual, were full of Servos. There are very few people on the walkways at any time and almost none at all in the mornings: Occasionally you run across tour groups, Outlanders from the Rural Lands, but now in the snow there was no one, it seemed, but me and the Servos. There were dozens of them, sweeping up the accumulations of litter, hosing down the streets with special chemicals to kill bacteria, operating the searchlights and beacons for the aircabs that passed overhead, doing dozens of other simple tasks. Several of them came up beside me and wiped the snow off my coat as I walked or held porto-heaters against my hands and face—so many, in fact, that I finally had to ask them to leave me alone. Servos are necessary and important and it's good to have a massive presence on the streets to deter crime, but sometimes they can be annoying.

As I walked I thought a little bit more about them. What was it like to be a Servo? Almost half the people in the New York megalopolis were and yet as far as I knew none of them had ever come forward to tell their story. Maybe that was because they had no story to tell; they simply had assigned functions or chosen functions, which they performed. Maybe the essence of being a Servo was just that: doing a minor job without thinking about it. If you really considered what you were or were doing, you might be unhappy because you'd have to admit that you had almost no function at all. Even Ralph, who had a responsible job as a Complex Fueltender, was little more than a semiskilled Servo; he could have been replaced in a day by one of the robotenders that were gathering dust and rust in storage, ready to be reactivated if the Servos were ever to strike. It was unlikely that they would, though; they were grateful for their jobs and had no reason not to be, even if some of them, like Ralph, did dream about bettering themselves and becoming celebrities like me.

A half hour passed before I realized that I was neither heading for Mort's offices nor wandering aimlessly. And yet I wasn't really surprised when I found myself approaching the

Ultradome. In the back of my conscious mind I'd known all the time that this was my destination; I'd gone to the Dome before, the night or day after a match when the lights were shut off and the crowds were gone and I could relive my victories in solitude. An empty stadium is entirely different from a filled one and not only because people aren't there.

The main entrance gates were locked up tight, of course. If I had wanted to go inside it would have been easy enough: Top-level pulpeteers are issued stadium pass cards, just as they're issued Unlimited Fuel cards. But I didn't really want to go into the Ultradome; I just wanted to be there in its shadow, to feel its towering and comforting presence nearby.

As I stood at the gates a crowd of Servos clustered around me with porto-heaters and hand-vacs and disposal cubes. "Come on," I said to them, "just leave me alone, okay?"

"We're only trying to help you," one of them said.

"The way you can help me is to disappear. If you don't I'll get in touch with the Agency and have you Full-Waged."

That's a way of saying that the Servo would be taken from his job and given his salary without having to work for it, and it's one of the most serious threats you can make. I don't like to threaten them but sometimes the only way you can have any peace is to be harsh. The Servos muttered and grumbled and shuffled around; within a minute, though, all of them were gone.

I put my hands on the cold metal of the gates and looked past the long runway into the stadium itself. There was no sign of any of the security Servos inside, fortunately, so I wouldn't have to deal with them.

A powerful feeling of isolation came over me as I looked at the enormous scoreboards, the rows and rows of empty seats, the great dome glistening under its weight of snow overhead. Dimly I could hear spectral echoes of the cheers, the applause that had rolled over me in waves yesterday; but they seemed muted, as if coming from a vast distance. Yesterday seemed to be something that had happened to another person in a different time.

I wondered if The Cranker felt this way too, the morning after *his* semifinal victory; if this, too, was what it was like to be old. Did he look back on what he'd done and feel that it had happened to some other person? The feeling was the strangest and saddest one I'd ever had in my life and I couldn't understand why it affected me so strongly or why my eyes seemed to grow moist. The wetness wasn't really tears, was it? No —it must have been from the cold and the wind-driven snow.

There were sudden sounds behind me: They made me blink rapidly several times and then turn. A long sleek black groundcar had drifted up a few meters away and a pair of faces were peering at me through the old two-way windows. Then one of the front doors slid open and a short man wearing a heavy coat and muffler came out. He shuddered at the cold—obviously an indoor person unaccustomed to weather. And in a not very polite way he beckoned to me.

"Hey," he said, "Rex Sackett. Come here."

I just looked at him. "Who are you? What do you want?"

"Come here, I said."

I didn't care for his tone and I thought I'd tell him so, too. He might have been a criminal, one of those who prey on unwary citizens in the streets, but they don't usually speak to their victims because they're afraid of having their voices preserved on a microrecorder and later checked through the police file of voiceprints. More likely he was either a scribe for one of the smaller and nastier New-Sport sheets or one of those belligerent fans who like to pick fights with well-known pulpeteers.

Cautiously, my hand hovering close to my tranq weapon, I went over to him. Just before I reached him he ducked down inside the groundcar; on impulse I leaned over to look in at him. That was when I got my first clear look at the second man sitting in the rear seat. He was wearing two coats, a muffler, a respirator, and filtration lenses over his eyes, but the face was still recognizable.

Huxtable.

"Hello, kid," he said. "Come in out of the cold."

"The hell I will," I said. "Have you been following me around? Is that it?"

"Yeah," Huxtable said, "and I wish it wasn't. I hate the outside on days like this. I'm going to get sick, that's what I'm going to do. Why do you go walking in the goddamn snow? Are you crazy?"

"What do you want?"

"That's not the question." Huxtable sneezed; the sound was hollowed and distorted by the respirator. He wiped his nose on his muffler and said, "The question is what do *you* want?"

"You to leave me alone," I said, "that's what I want."

"A nice comfortable life or a lot of pain?" Huxtable said as if he hadn't heard me. "Five million dollars and plenty of ease, or a lousy Prose Bowl trophy and plenty of trouble? Which is it going to be, kiddo?"

"You're trying to coerce me again!"

"You're a smart kid. Maybe."

"Goddamnit," the man behind the controls of the car said, "I'm freezing my ass off in here. I can't get the heater to stay up. Will you stop bantering with him and get it over with?"

"All right, Rollo, just take it easy," Huxtable said soothingly. He looked back at me. "You can do this the easy way, Sackett, or you can do it the hard way. The choice is yours. So what's your decision?"

"I already told you that yesterday. It's still the same."

"You're liable to get hurt, kid, don't you see that? We're not just playing around here; we mean business."

"Are you threatening me now?"

"Call it what you want. How about getting in and we'll go talk this over where it's nice and warm. We'll work out the details—"

"The only detail I'm going to work out with you is *this,*" I said angrily, and before I even realized what I was doing I had my tranq weapon in my hand and pointed at Huxtable's runny nose. The man in the front seat, Rollo, stiffened and seemed to want to reach inside his coat; his hand hovered near the top two buttons. But then he just sat there, poised, watching me and waiting.

The tranq weapon was making Huxtable nervous; a little film of sweat formed on his forehead, iced there above the filtration lenses. "Put it away, kid," he said.

"No," I said, "I'm not going to put it away. I'm going to shoot you with it and then call the police if you don't leave me alone and stop trying to coerce me. I'm not going to throw the Prose Bowl; I'm an honest pro, not a damned crooked Editor like you."

"You'll be sorry for this, Sackett."

"You'll be even sorrier if I put one of these darts through your eye," I told him.

Huxtable and Rollo exchanged a long look. "All right," Huxtable said in a resigned voice, "I guess we'll have to do it your way."

"Damn right you will," I said.

"I wasn't talking to you, kid," he said, and Rollo reached out suddenly and flicked a button on the control panel; the door began to slide shut, almost pinning my arm before I could jerk it back. Then the groundcar's engine roared and the machine squealed away, vanishing almost instantly behind the screen of falling snow.

I stood staring down the empty street, still holding the tranq weapon in my hand, shivering with emotion now instead of with cold. The walkways were empty too, I realized; no one had seen the incident, no one had been around to help me if I'd needed help. Not even the Servos, because I'd scared them all away.

I felt more alone in that moment than I'd ever felt before.

8

Mort's offices were in a Sky Complex in the Inner Southern Sector, on Avenue the Honorable Richard Milhous Nixon near the ruins of the old and tiny Empire State Building. I went straight there from the Ultradome, not walking this time but riding in an express aircab. And I brooded the whole way. Damn Huxtable and that Rollo person! They were menaces, that was what they were, trying to corrupt one of the few good and dignified institutions left in the world. Throw the Prose Bowl? It was unthinkable, it was . . . well, it was *un-American.*

In the chute on the way down to the 259th floor I told myself that this time I was going to insist we report the bribe offers and threats to the authorities. Let the police harass me; let the scribes and TriDim types like Penn insinuate anything they wanted. I just didn't care. The integrity of the Prose Bowl, of every prosemaker who ever sat down behind a machine in a professional face-off, was at stake here.

The Morgandahl Prose Fic Agency occupied a two-room suite, which was evidence right there of how successful Mort was; two-room suites cost ninety thousand dollars a month nowadays and were at a premium in number because of that high rent. Diana Pollard was sitting behind her desk in the outer cubicle, typing on one of the new compact, self-cleaning computers, when I came in. She looked a little tired—her emerald-streaked red hair hung limply over the winged shoulders of her tunic and there were dark smudges under her eyes—and she seemed a little grumpy too, as if she'd spent a bad or at least an irritating night.

"Hello, Diana," I said. "Is Mort in?"

"He's in *this morning*," she said in an ironic sort of way, as if she'd expected him to be in somewhere last night too. "I'll see if he's busy."

She switched on the intercom and spoke into it. It struck me that this was somehow a little unfair, that even though I was going to the Prose Bowl and was one of Mort's top moneymaking clients, I still had to wait in the outer office instead of being ushered right in to his private room. But Mort, like every agent, has his own way of doing things and I know that whatever he does is for my own good. Still, after the incident with Huxtable and Rollo, I felt pretty nervous and impatient. The fact was, I was a little bit scared.

Diana turned back to me and said, "He'll be out in just a minute or two. Why don't you sit down?"

"I'll stand instead, thanks," I said. "I'm too upset to sit right now; I've had kind of a hard morning."

"I wish I'd had a hard night," Diana said. She really did have a bitter expression on her face.

I paced around, looking at things on the walls while Diana went back to typing on the computer. Mort's offices, both the reception room and his own cubicle, were interesting in that they weren't filled with twentieth-century prose or even objects that have much to do with modern pulpeteering; instead they're decorated with Old-Sport artifacts from the mid-1900s—plaques and mementos from what Mort once called, strangely, "the last era of true sport"; autographed baseballs and pictures of athletes throwing footballs and antique bowling pins and tennis raquets. I've always found the implements of Old-Sport sort of bizarre, but Mort accumulated them at great expense and they apparently meant something to him. Once, when I asked him why he kept them in his offices instead of prose materials, he said it was because prose was too personal and Old-Sport artifacts were just trivia for the amusement of his clients. That didn't seem quite right to me—what could entertain a pulpeteer more than TriDim photos of himself in action or copies of his best prose efforts in competition? But then, as Mort has reminded me many times, I'm still relatively new to this business and there's a lot I don't understand yet.

It wasn't easy to keep calm while I waited and I guess I did enough restless pacing to distract Diana. Usually she doesn't react to me at all, but after awhile she looked up and said, "What's wrong with you? Can't you stand still?"

"Gee, I'm sorry, Diana," I said. "It's just that I'm really upset."

"Why don't you take a tranq?"

"I don't have any."

"Well, I'd give you one of mine but I used them all last night."

"Were you excited over something?"

"I sure wasn't excited *under* anything," Diana said bitterly. She went back to typing on her computer.

It seemed odd that she hadn't bothered to congratulate me on my semifinal victory over Ollie Garbowitz yesterday. She wasn't a very demonstrative person, though; and whatever she was so bitter about seemed to be occupying all her thoughts.

Mort opened the inner door finally and looked out at me. He was wearing a Shakespearean outfit today, complete with Elizabethan *hauts-de-chausses*, and he looked pretty dapper. "Sorry I took so long, kid," he said. "I was tied up."

"Maybe *that* would have worked," Diana muttered.

Mort glared at her and said, "Shut up."

"Up?" she said. "I didn't know the word was in your vocabulary."

Mort's face got kind of orange-red and he breathed heavily through his mouth, puffing out his cheeks. Then he fumbled his pink pass card out of his waistcoat and waved it at Diana in a menacing way. "You'd better watch yourself, person," he said. "I don't want any more from you."

"You're telling me you don't?" Diana said bitterly.

Mort made a growling sound. Then he pushed me into his private office and slammed the door so hard some baseballs on the wall wobbled inside their frames and almost popped loose.

I said, "Are you having some sort of problem, Mort?"

"Problem?" he snapped. "What the hell makes you think I'm having a problem? I'm not having a problem. It's just a temporary thing, that's all. Temporary."

"What is?"

"Never mind. Forget it." He gestured me to one of his clients' chairs. "It's a tough life sometimes, kid," he said. "Just be happy you're not in this end of the prose racket, that you can write your own ticket. And just make sure that girl of yours doesn't tell you what to do or how to do it. You do what you want to do. While you still can."

"Sure, Mort."

He seemed to cheer up as he sat down behind his massive desk. "Some match last night, wasn't it? The Cranker was in top form, but I think he used up everything he had just so he could get through and into the Bowl. He won't have much left next week."

"I hope you're right," I said.

"You bet I am." Mort reached inside his doublet and produced five orange-red superjet tickets, the same color his complexion had been. "Got everybody courtesy-booked for flights out to Greater Los Angeles," he said, handing me four of the tickets. "I'm leaving tonight; your reservation is set for Thursday. Sally and your folks, too."

"How come you're leaving tonight?"

"So I can line up a few things for us. I think I can get you an Informational and maybe a TriDim entertainment spot after the Bowl. If you win, of course. But I'm not worried about that; you'll win."

"Mort," I said, "I didn't come up here to talk about the match." I took a deep breath. "Huxtable approached me again a little while ago. He threatened me right out this time; either I agree to throw the Face-Off or something will happen to me."

He scowled. "Okay, kid, what happened?"

"This is *serious,* Mort," I said.

"I know it's serious. So tell me what happened."

The words came pouring out of me, all the details and as much verbatim dialogue as I could remember. "They mean business," I said, finishing. "There's no telling what they might do."

"They won't do a damned thing," Mort said. "They wouldn't dare. You're a public figure; they'd have to be crazy to try harming you."

"I'm not so sure about that," I said darkly. "Mort, I think we ought to go to the authorities right away."

"The authorities?"

"Before everything gets out of hand."

Mort did some ruminating. "Things won't get out of hand," he said at length. "I'll see to that."

"You will? How?"

"Just leave that to me. I'll handle it."

"But—"

He reached over and patted my hand. "Listen," he said, "we've been together through the best and the worst for six years now. I've been working with you since you were eighteen, a wet-behind-the-ears kid who didn't know Horse Opera from Quality Lit, a narrative hook from a delayed revelation. I got you all the way to the Prose Bowl and pretty soon you're going to be champion, but you've got to trust me. Have I ever steered you wrong?"

"No, Mort. Only—"

"This is a tough business," he said over my objection. "I've been in it for twenty-five years myself and even I don't know all the angles. Things are changing all the time, new kids are coming up, old prose forms are being realigned; just when you think you know everything they throw a new angle at you. You listen to me, that's what I'm here for, that's what you're paying me forty-five percent of your income for. I'll make sure Huxtable and this Rollo character don't bother you anymore. All right?"

"Well . . . if you say so. . . ."

"Okay. So go home and exercise that leg of yours and

keep the vi-com on disconnect and work on your narrative hooks in all the categories, so you'll be ready for whatever they give you on Sunday. And stay away from the scribes and those bastards from TriDim; don't talk to anybody except Sally and your folks. Thursday I'll arrange for an aircab to pick all of you up and get you to the skyport in time for your flight."

I wanted to argue some more, to plead my case more strongly for going to the police; but I've never been able to take an aggressive stance with Mort. He's older and wiser than me and I was always taught to respect my elders. He'd said he would handle things, keep Huxtable and Rollo from harassing me again, and I had to believe that he'd be true to his word. You had to have complete faith in your agent. If you didn't, what was the use of having an agent in the first place?

Mort showed me to the door and clapped me on the shoulder and gave me a reassuring smile. Diana wasn't at her desk; he seemed relieved to see that. "Take care of yourself now, kid," he said, and closed the door gently but firmly as soon as I was through it.

I felt as though I were moving through an abandoned and somehow familiar room as I crossed to the suite's entrance. More and more lately I seemed to have these curious moments of abstraction, where the familiar seemed to become another aspect of the unknown. It was as if once having practiced living my life, I was now compelled to relive it in circumstances that were just a little different—as though life itself was the pulpeteer's deadliest enemy: a second draft.

Halfway down to the chute Diana turned a corner from the restrooms and we nearly bumped into each other. "Well," she said, "I see he finished you off in a hurry."

"Finished me off?"

"He's good at finishing off in a hurry," she said bitterly. "When he can get started in the first place, that is."

"I don't understand," I said.

"Neither do I. Good luck in the Prose Bowl, anyway," she said, and quickly walked away.

I rode down in the chute feeling puzzled and a little lost.

Outside it was still snowing, but the flakes now were light and hard and sparkling, like solidified crystals of Fuel. I started walking again, not heading toward my own Complex because I didn't want to face being alone there just yet—not heading anywhere, I thought, just walking aimlessly. Except that I *wasn't* walking aimlessly; I had a destination in mind and it wasn't long before I realized it.

There was one person I could talk to who might understand the way I felt. One person I wanted to be with just now more than anybody else.

There was Sally.

9

It was fifteen hundred hours when I got to Sally's wine-red Complex in the Upper Western Sector. The Servo on the door inserted my guest card into the Checkpoint computer, and when the printout said I was qualified, he called Sally's apartment on the Complex intercom to announce me. Two minutes later I was on the 316th floor and was passing my hand through the light beam for the door chimes and the inside security scanner.

"Hello, Rex," Sally said when she opened the door. "I thought you were the Servo from the Concertium."

"What?"

"I mean when the call came from Checkpoint that I had a visitor. Someone is supposed to bring over the scores for the Ravel 'Daphnis and Chloe' for me to collate for tonight's performance."

"You seem really delighted to see me," I said.

"It's just that I was expecting the Servo. Come in."

She stepped aside for me. Right away I could sense some distance in her manner; she usually greets me with a squeeze of the hand and a nice kiss on the forehead, but she didn't touch me this time. I walked past her into the L-shaped single room that was her apartment. She didn't have many furnishings and the decorations were all in musical patterns: notes on the curtains and upholstery, little treble and bass clefs patterned on the walls. Old musical instruments such as mandolins and guitars and saxophones hung on the walls on both sides of the L. I had always hated that apartment, though I'd never let on about my feelings to Sally, and seeing it again now made me wonder all over again if her idea of us blending our interests and life-styles was going to work out. Just the thought of living in a place with all that musical junk around me was depressing.

We went into the longer angle of the L and I sat down in one of the chairs. And as soon as I did I felt that lost and lonely feeling press in on me. "I need to talk to you, Sally," I said. "I . . . well, I'm in some trouble."

"Trouble?" she said. "I should say you are, Rex, and it's about time you admitted it—"

"No, you don't understand. Something's happened— something *awful.*"

Her expression changed, became concerned; she sat in the chair next to me. "What is it?"

I told her everything about the two meetings with Huxtable, about how I'd gone to Mort's offices and what he'd said. "I guess he's right and I've got to let him handle things," I said, "but I just can't help being mixed up and worried."

"He's *not* right," Sally said. Anger flickered behind the concern in her eyes. "Those men sound ugly and dangerous to me; your life could be in jeopardy, Rex, you could be *killed.*"

"I'm not going to be killed," I said, but the thought made me shiver a little. "Mort won't let me down—"

"Why are you so sure about that?"

"Because I am. He's not only my agent, he's my friend. He knows what's best for me, even if I don't. What do I know about anything?"

"You'd know a lot if only you weren't so trusting and naive."

"Naive?"

"Yes," Sally said. "You'd know that all Mort Morgandahl cares about is himself, for one thing. He doesn't care about you at all."

"That's not true!"

"It is. It is true."

"Sally, I know you don't like Mort but that's no reason to —"

"I don't like Mort and I don't like pulpeteering either. Neither would you if you saw it the way I do. But you're so blinded by the glamour and the money and the competition that you can't see how demeaning and terrible it really is."

"Demeaning and terrible?"

"Yes."

"I'm going to the Prose Bowl," I said, "I'm going to be on National TriDim with fifty or sixty million people watching when I face-off against The Cranker. The championship prize is two and a half million dollars, Sally. Is that demeaning and terrible? *Two and a half million dollars!*"

"That's all you can think about, isn't it? Money and glory, just like I said. Well, what about what New-Sport is doing to you as a human being? You don't have a single friend anymore, you spend most of your time alone training because those are Mort's orders, you don't see me or your parents except on special occasions. You're angry and irritable and preoccupied all the time and you drink too much Fuel—much too much Fuel. And now you've gotten involved with a bunch of criminals who are threatening your life."

I was getting angry all over again. What this was was another lecture from someone who thought he knew all about me: Mort, Penn, the scribes, Dad, Sally. They all knew how I should manage my life, except that they didn't know anything at all. None of them were pulpeteers, none of them knew what it was like to go out and face a blank sheet of paper that you had to fill up with words disgorged from somewhere deep inside you.

"I don't want to listen to any more of this," I said. "You're my girl, but you just don't understand."

"I understand more than you think I do, Rex."

"Sure," I said. "Sure. What do you want me to do, then? Withdraw from the Prose Bowl? Pack my belongings and run away somewhere and hide? Wouldn't Huxtable and Rollo love that!"

"I don't want you to withdraw," Sally said. "But after the

Prose Bowl is over I want you to retire from competition, whether you win or lose. You'll have enough money either way; we'll be able to live comfortably."

"Where? Not here in New York, that's for sure."

"No. Someplace else, someplace where we can start a whole new life."

"Like Luna Colony, I suppose."

"Yes. Exactly. We could go to Luna Colony—"

"And live underground like a couple of damned rodents," I said. I was on my feet now and so was she, and we were glaring at each other like enemies instead of lovers; but I was too furious to care right then. "No, I won't do it. I won't quit New-Sport; I'm not a quitter, Sally. And I won't run away to Luna Colony under any circumstances, not even with you."

"Maybe you won't have to worry about that."

"Worry about what?"

"Going *anywhere* with me," she said angrily. "Marrying me or ever even seeing me again."

"You want to walk out of my life? Is that it? Well, go ahead then. See if I care. See if I care what the hell you do!"

She raised her hand and I think she might have slapped me if the musical door chimes hadn't sounded at just that moment. Both of us stood motionless for three or four seconds; then Sally half-spun away from me, skirts swirling, and disappeared in hard unfeminine strides beyond the shorter angle of the L. I went over and started to sit down again, changed my mind, and just stood staring at the snow falling outside the window.

I wasn't thinking about anything; I was too upset for any logical progression of thoughts. But at the back of my mind was the perception that the caller was the Servo Sally had been expecting from the Concertium. And yet I also had the vague perception that it was odd the Checkpoint Servo downstairs hadn't buzzed to announce a visitor, the way he had with me. . . .

Sally screamed.

It was a shrill terrified cry and it whirled me around from the window, sent me rushing around the corner toward the front door. What I saw there, just inside the opening, made me cry out with a mixture of fear and outrage: Sally was struggling in the grasp of two men, one of them with his hand clapped across her mouth, the other clutching at her ankles and trying to lift her inside a collapsible porto-carrier.

The first man was Rollo, the driver of the groundcar outside the Ultradome.

The second man was Huxtable.

Everything that happened in the next few seconds had a kind of surreal quality, nightmarish, as if I weren't actually involved in it but were *writing* it instead in one of my most intense face-offs. As if it were nothing more than a fast-action narrative scene, told in the third person about a protagonist named Rex Sackett. . . .

HE LET LOOSE A BELLOW OF FURY AND PLUNGED TOWARD THE THREE STRUGGLING FIGURES NEAR THE OPEN DOOR. HUXTABLE RELEASED SALLY'S LEGS, TURNED TO MEET SACKETT'S CHARGE, AN EVIL GRIN TWISTING HIS VENAL FEATURES. SACKETT LAUNCHED A TERRIBLE BLOW, LIKE A GREAT AND POWERFUL SPRING UNCOILING, BUT HE WAS OFF-BALANCE AND HIS FIST CONNECTED WITH NOTHING BUT AIR AS HUXTABLE SIDESTEPPED. THE CORRUPT EDITOR RETALIATED, CRACKING THE YOUNG PULPETEER ACROSS THE CHEEK WITH THE HEEL OF ONE PALM. PAIN ERUPTED VOLCANICALLY, BLURRING SACKETT'S VISION WITH PATTERNS OF RED AND YELLOW DOTS.

THEN THE TWO OF THEM WERE GRAPPLING, LOCKED IN MORTAL COMBAT. BUT HUXTABLE WAS STRONGER AND MORE EXPERIENCED AT HAND-TO-HAND TACTICS, DOUBTLESS FROM HIS CRIMINAL ASSOCIATIONS, AND IT WAS ONLY SECONDS BEFORE SACKETT WAS HURLED AGAINST THE WALL WITH VICIOUS FORCE, SO VICIOUS THAT WHEN HE HEARD A CRACKING SOUND HE BELIEVED AT FIRST THAT IT WAS HIS SPINE.

THROUGH A HAZE OF SWEAT AND TEARS, HE

SAW ROLLO HEAVE SALLY INTO THE AIR, BRACING
HER STRUGGLING BODY AGAINST HIS, AND THEN
SHOVE HER DOWN PITILESSLY INSIDE THE PORTO-
CARRIER. SACKETT'S RAGE REKINDLED AND HE
BELLOWED AGAIN AS ROLLO BEGAN TO PUSH THE
BOX OUT INTO THE CORRIDOR. HE LUNGED FOR-
WARD, TRYING TO HURL HIMSELF PAST HUXTABLE
TO SAVE THE HELPLESS GIRL HE LOVED.

BUT HE DIDN'T MAKE IT. HIS ATTENTION WAS
ON ROLLO AND THE CARRIER AND HE DIDN'T SEE
WHAT HUXTABLE WAS DOING UNTIL IT WAS TOO
LATE. THE SWINISH FELON HAD SEIZED AN EXPEN-
SIVE OLD MANDOLIN FROM SALLY'S WALL, HER
MOST PRIZED POSSESSION, AND WAS RAISING IT
HIGH OVER HIS HEAD AS SACKETT THUNDERED
PAST. THEN THE INSTRUMENT DESCENDED WITH
TREMENDOUS FORCE, LANDING SQUARELY ON TOP
OF THE POOR PROSEMAKER'S SKULL. THERE WAS A
TWANGING OF STRINGS, AS IF FROM FAR AWAY, AND
AN EXPLOSION OF MORE RED AND YELLOW DOTS
BEHIND HIS EYES; A SENSATION OF FALLING OVER-
TOOK HIM.

THEN THERE WAS NOTHING AT ALL.
REX SACKETT WAS DOWN AND OUT.

PART TWO

Saving Sally

1

It was dark when I woke up and for a minute or two I didn't know where I was or what had happened. My head felt as if I had drunk four containers of Fuel and then gone to sleep for awhile. Then I remembered, and I staggered up off the carpet and lurched around the apartment, switching on all the lights, looking inside closets with an increasing sense of panic.

Sally was gone.

I found the note they'd left when I came back to the front door; it was on one of the decorative music stands near the smashed mandolin. The words were printed in a childish hand on the back of a musical scoresheet and they said:

> We have your girl. If you want her back alive you'd better do exactly what you're told. Go home and sit beside your vi-com. Don't contact the police or anybody else or you'll never see Sally again. We'll be in touch.

That was all.

My hands were shaking so bad by the time I finished reading it that the scoresheet slipped out of my fingers and fluttered to the floor. When I bent down to pick it up I saw that there was something else on the carpeting nearby, half-hidden under the smashed mandolin—something that hadn't been there earlier. I fished it out. And what it was was a Complex pass card, but not an ordinary one; it wasn't color-coded, just sort of frost-hued, and it was a little smaller than normal in size. I thought that it was probably one of the very few and strictly controlled cards given to upper-echelon government officials and government security agents, which can be used to clear the bearer through any Checkpoint computer in any Sky Complex and to open any apartment or office door.

Had Huxtable lost it when I was grappling with him? It was illegal for any non-government-affiliated citizen to have a Special pass card, but there had been cases where ones were stolen and used for nefarious purposes by criminals. And it would explain how Huxtable and Rollo had gotten into Sally's Complex without being questioned or at least announced by the Checkpoint Servo.

The one thing it didn't explain, though, was where those two evil bastards had taken her.

I shoved the Special card and the kidnap note into the pocket of my tunic. Then, instinctively, I went to Sally's vicom, switched on both audio and visual, and dialed Mort's office. Diana came on after several seconds; she was wearing her coat and the same bitter expression of earlier in the afternoon.

"Oh, hello, Rex," she said. "I was just about to go home."

"Home?"

"It's seventeen thirty hours," Diana said. "I didn't get any overtime last night, so I'm not putting in any here tonight."

"Is Mort still there?"

"Mort went to Greater L.A."

I made an involuntary groaning sound; I'd forgotten all about him leaving tonight instead of later in the week. "God, Diana," I said, "I've got to talk to him. I've got to! Where's he staying out there? You've got to tell me."

She didn't say anything for several seconds; she seemed to be studying me. Then her expression softened a little and she said, "You're really upset, aren't you?"

"Yes. Yes I am."

"Well . . . maybe Mort hasn't left just yet, after all."

"What?"

"Maybe he's still in New York."

"You mean at the Skyport?"

"No, I mean still in New York," she said. "Maybe his ticket is for tomorrow, you know?" She shrugged. "Half the time he gets things screwed up."

"Do you really think there's a chance?"

"There's always a chance for a nice kid like you."

"I'm going to try him at home, then."

"You do that," Diana said. "Not me, though; I think I've had just about enough of Mort Morgandahl. In fact I think he's a Servo-head."

"A Servo-head? Diana, why are you being so hard on Mort?"

"Hard on Mort?" she said bitterly. "That's the best laugh I've had all day." And she switched off at her end and the screen went dark.

I called Mort's home number and waited through at least twenty rings: no answer. So much for the little hope Diana had given me. I thought about calling Mom and Dad, but I knew that wouldn't do any good at all. Mom would just go to pieces and start crying and Dad wouldn't know what to do or say. The truth is, he can't handle a crisis; he goes straight for the Fuel when one comes along. All he'd end up doing would be to tell me to call in the authorities, kid, and he'd never even consider that it might get Sally killed.

Kid, I thought. Diana had just called me that, and so did Dad and Mort and just about everybody else—as if I were too young to really see or understand things. It was starting to rankle me.

I slammed down the vi-com handset in helplessness and frustration. Now what are you going to do? I asked myself. Come on, kid, what are you going to do?

Go home and sit beside your vi-com. Don't contact the police or anybody else or you'll never see Sally again.

The words from the kidnap note seemed to roll across my mind like prose printout across one of the great boards in the Ultradome. I felt blood rise in my cheeks, making them feel fiery with sudden shame. The instructions in the note were explicit, and I hadn't paid any attention to them; the first thing I'd done, the very first thing, was to go to the vi-com and call Mort's office.

I had jeopardized Sally's life—again.

What a fool I'd been! What a damned *kid!* Ever since yesterday I'd been dealing with racketeers so corrupt they'd try to fix the Prose Bowl, so daring they'd approach a pulpeteer in a public Fuel lounge and on a public street, so cruel they'd commit kidnapping and aggravated assault with a mandolin to get what they wanted. And how had I reacted? I'd gone to Mort twice, let him talk me out of calling the authorities twice; I'd carried on as though Huxtable and Rollo would go away and everything would be all right if I just ignored the situation, as though I were dealing with reasonable people instead of mobsters. And then, to top it all off, I'd just disobeyed instructions with my Sally's life hanging in the balance.

It's time for you to grow up, damn it, I told myself. Time for you to start accepting some responsibility before it's too late. Do what you should have done immediately. Don't waste any more time!

I hurried out of there, shutting the apartment door behind me, and took the chute up to the aircab station on the roof. It was still snowing and the cold air cleared my head, made me feel a little better. While I was waiting for a cab I asked some of the Servos if they'd seen Sally or two men with a porto-carrier; none of them had. They must have left the Complex at ground level, maybe by one of the side entrances to avoid being seen.

And then what? Where had they taken her?

In my mind I could see her face, soft and sweet-smiling when we were alone together. But I could also see it, like shadow images, the way it had looked when we were arguing, saying those terrible words to each other, and when she was terrified and struggling in the grasp of Huxtable and Rollo. Those images made me ache inside, and filled me with remorse and a kind of self-hatred too: How could I have done this to Sally, who loved me and only wanted the best for me?

But then I forced myself to jam all the guilt and pain and confusion into a small pocket of my mind; I had to stay calm, I had to keep a tight reign on my control. The burden of Sally's safety rested on my shoulders; I would have to see this through by myself, make all the decisions and do whatever else was necessary myself to bring her back to me. No Mort this time, no Mom or Dad or anybody else. Just Rex Sackett— all alone.

A cab came finally and I got inside and told the three Servos working the controls where I wanted to go. The ride through the snowy night to my Complex was a blur; it seemed I could hear Sally's voice in the sound of the engines, above the mindless chattering of the Servos. But when it ended at last I was still holding on to my calm, and even more resolved not to take any kind of action from now on until I'd given it careful thought first.

The first thing I did after I entered my apartment was to make sure the vi-com was connected and working okay. I cursed myself for not putting on the message tape before leaving earlier; if I had, and if Huxtable had already tried to get in touch with me, there might be a message waiting right now. But I didn't use the tape much. About the only people who ever called were occasional scribes or TriDim announcers wanting interviews, even though they were supposed to clear permission through Mort first.

I'd left a container of Fuel on one of the tables and I caught myself looking at it as I shrugged out of my coat. As nervous and tensed up as I was, four or five ounces of Fuel were just what I needed to soothe me out. Only I didn't dare take even one ounce. I had to have a clear head, and with the pressure I was under there was the possibility that the Fuel would hit me wrong, give me a sudden and crippling overload. It had happened to me that way a couple of times before, like after my close quarterfinal loss to The Hackensack Hack last season; I'd been sick in bed for three days then with Fuel overload, and I'd only had maybe ten or eleven ounces over a four-hour period.

I sat down on the couch and stared at the vi-com, willing it to ring. Nothing happened. My chronometer said the time was 2015, which meant that more than five hours had passed since Sally had been kidnapped. Why didn't they call, damn them? What were they waiting for?

The silence in the apartment seemed to grow louder, more acute, with each passing second, so that I imagined I could hear the snowflakes slapping against the plastoid windowpanes. I stood up and began to pace, but the silence just kept on getting worse, almost suffocating, as if the room were being wrapped up like a cocoon with meter after meter of invisible silk. Finally, in desperation, I ran to the TriDim and switched it on: If I didn't have sound, any kind of sound, I was going to start making it myself by screaming.

And wouldn't you know that the first human face and first human voice to come on would both belong to Harmon Penn. He was doing live analysis and commentary over taped replays of both semifinal matches, building interest for the Prose Bowl. I listened to him talking about The Cranker's magnificent performance against Fast-Action Eddie, how Culp seemed to have finally beaten the personal devils that had kept him from making it to the championship round throughout his long career. Penn was snide and nasty about those so-called personal devils and made wiggling motions with his eyebrows and mouth that intimated they were scandalous and he'd love to reveal them if only he could.

Then he talked about me, saying that I was a relatively raw and inexperienced kid ("kid" again) and how this might be the easiest, least competitive Prose Bowl in recent memory. The high point of this year's competition had been between The Cranker and Fast-Action Eddie, he said, and Culp would slide right through now to an easy victory over a demoralized opponent. That was just how he put it: "demoralized opponent." Which was probably true, I thought with bitter irony; I felt pretty demoralized, all right.

I got up and switched to another channel, which was playing a horse opera with lots of shooting and whooping and gave me the sound I needed without making me think. I didn't want to think anymore, especially not about The Cranker or the Prose Bowl or Harmon goddamn Penn. The way Penn talked was really getting to me. It was as if all of New-Sport, including pulpeteers like me and Culp, were just props or script material so he could put on his show day after day and week after week; as if we didn't matter at all.

More time passed. I took out my pipe, thinking that a smoke might help me to relax, but I had run out of tobacco. And I didn't dare leave the apartment even to go down to the Fuel lounge for a fresh package. I would have settled for quasi-tobacco, only I didn't have any of that either. You couldn't buy it in my neighborhood and it was only for the Servos anyway, the same as Quasi-Fuel; nobody who could afford the real stuff ever bothered with it because it was so cheaply made and so weak-tasting.

So I just sat and stared around at the TriDim horse opera and fidgeted, waiting for something to happen. And in spite of myself I started to think about Sally alone in a room somewhere with Huxtable and Rollo, maybe tied up but in any case totally at their mercy. I imagined them laughing and taunting her, torturing her in some way, doing things even more terrible to her pure young body. That started me trembling all over again, made me reconsider going to the authorities. But I knew I couldn't bring myself to do that. They'd be liable to do something that would alert Huxtable, and then he'd make good on his threat to kill Sally, and then maybe he'd come after me and kill me too.

I stood up again and paced.

I sat down again and stared at the container of Fuel.

I looked at my chronometer for the dozenth or hundredth time: twenty-one hundred hours exactly.

I started to reach forward to switch the TriDim to another channel—

The vi-com bell went off.

The sound of it would have made me jump half a meter if the horse opera hadn't been blaring away; as it was I jerked and a chill went down my back. I lunged up and almost tripped over my feet getting to the vi-com. I switched on both audio and visual, but the screen remained dark; whoever was calling hadn't put on the visual at his end.

Huxtable, I thought as I said "Hello? Hello?" into the handset. My heart was thumping like crazy; a sudden sweat made the palms of my hands slick and oily.

And seconds later I heard his cruel voice say, "You been a good little boy, Sackett? Follow instructions like you were told?"

"I followed them," I said.

"Looks like you're alone. Are you?"

"Yes. I didn't tell anybody what happened."

"Good. You're kind of a stupid kid, but you're learning."

"Is Sally all right? You . . . you haven't hurt her?"

"She's just fine," Huxtable said. "So far, anyway."

"Let me talk to her. Please."

"Uh-uh."

"But then how do I know she's all right?"

"You'll just have to take my word for it."

I gripped the handset harder, strangling it as if it were Huxtable's neck. "What do you want me to do?" I asked.

"You know the answer to that, kid."

"Throw the Prose Bowl. Pretend to get another hamstring pull in the third quarter and then withdraw."

"You got it," Huxtable said. "So you're going to keep on being a good little boy, right? Keep on doing just what you're told so you can have your girl back in one piece."

"Yes. But I want to see Sally first, and not just on vi-com. I want to talk to her in person."

Huxtable didn't say anything. Or maybe he did and I missed it; there seemed to be some sort of banging interference on the line. I started to repeat what I'd said, a little less boldly, but he cut me off. "Okay," he said, "maybe that can be arranged."

"When?"

"Tell you what. We'll have a meeting tonight, one hour from now—just you and me and Sally."

"Where?"

"How about the Ultradome. Say D Section tunnel, on the southwest side."

"Why the Ultradome?"

"Why not?" Huxtable said. "It's a place we both know and we can have a nice little talk there without being disturbed." He paused. "Just one thing, kid—"

"Yes?"

"You'd better come alone. If you bring the nabbers, Sally'll be the first one to get it."

There was a magnified clicking sound as he switched off.

I put the handset down and dried my palms on the front of my tunic. The idea of going alone to the Ultradome on a dark snowy night like this, facing Huxtable and maybe Rollo too, was a little frightening. What if they kidnapped me too? Or beat me up or something to make sure I did what they wanted? But I couldn't think about possibilities like those; I had to go, I had to try to save Sally any way I could, and that was all there was to it.

Grimly I unsheathed my tranq weapon, checked the load and set it for maximum sedative at maximum velocity. Then I threw on my coat, resisted an almost overpowering urge to reach for the container of Fuel, and hurried out of there.

2

The southwestern side of the Ultradome had a lonely, desolate look: no people on the sidewalks, no groundcars in the street or aircabs in the misty snow overhead, no lights anywhere in the stadium, no neon-lit Informationals to color the heavy black. Snowdrifts blocked part of the locked entrance gate; beyond the electro-mesh, the shadows looked ominous and motionless, like dark things waiting for prey.

I stood motionless myself for several seconds, studying the bleak surroundings, shivering inside my coat. I was scared, there was no use in lying to myself about that; but determination and a thin glow of anger helped to keep me calm. So did the tranq weapon, which I kept clenching inside my coat pocket.

When I was sure I was alone I moved up close to the gate and peered through into the shadows. But there wasn't anything to see. Maybe Huxtable was here already and maybe he wasn't; the time was only 2145 hours. The security Servos would be somewhere inside, but probably no more than a half dozen of them on night duty—and on a bitter cold night like this they'd no doubt be huddled together in the Security Office on the north side, rather than out patrolling the stadium.

In the aircab on the way from my Complex I'd considered contacting the security Servos, telling them what was going on and asking them to help me. But that was no better an idea than going to the police. What if Huxtable was watching somewhere and saw me? What if one of the Servos had been bribed to watch out for just that sort of thing? No, I couldn't take the chance—not with so much at stake, not with Sally's life. There had to be some other way to save her, some way that depended only on me. Some way that didn't involve throwing the Prose Bowl on Sunday, because at heart I was a true pulpeteer and even to save the girl I loved I wasn't sure if I could go through with such a terrible act of betrayal.

I took out my Ultradome pass card and slid it into the slot above the computer-lock; there was a soft whirring as the electro-mesh current was shut off and the latch released. I had one more look around me, saw nothing but the same snowbound emptiness. Then I pushed the gate open and eased inside, closing it again after me.

The stadium heating units were shut off at night, to conserve energy as required by law; it was as cold in the dark areaway as it was outside. And so still the air had a brittle quality, like thin ice about to crack. Even though I moved ahead slowly, on the balls of my feet, each step seemed to set up a faint hollow echo in the blackness.

I thought about using the pocket infraflash I always carry, but I was afraid of alerting the security Servos. Besides, I'd been coming to the Ultradome for New-Sport matches for almost fifteen years now and I knew my way around the areaways pretty well. So I was able to orient myself and head in the right direction without light.

As I threaded my way toward the D Section tunnel, the metal-and-glass detectors for the screening of fans entering the stadium loomed as clotted masses of shadow. So did the vendor stands for Fuel and Quasi-Fuel, for peanuts and old-fashioned frankfurters; I could smell their lingering odors on the cold air. But I didn't stumble over anything and the only noises I made—the only noises anywhere—were those of my footfalls. If Huxtable or anyone else was in this section, he wasn't moving around near enough for me to hear him.

It seemed like a long time before the lighter black of the tunnel entrance appeared ahead. I quickened my pace a little, reached the entrance, and started up the ramp, staying in close to one wall. As I climbed, the inner stadium began to materialize: the curving rows of empty seats, each one form-fitting and made of undamageable plastoid; the high smooth dome, transparent most of the time but now a solid gray-black parabola under a clinging coat of snow; the field itself, with its sideline benches and Editors' tables, with the two competition machines facing each other across the Line, shuttered now and draped in shadow; the massive scoreboards staring down blindly from their lofty positions at either end.

A shiver rippled through me as I stopped at the point where the ramp widened out and blended into parallel escalator belts. Part of it was the unknown—what I would say and do when I saw Huxtable and Sally, what he would say and do, how I would get her out of his and Rollo's miserable clutches. But part of it was the *known* too: the great stadium, so familiar and yet so different and eerie-looking in its nighttime desertion.

It was as if the Ultradome were some sort of huge beast looming up around me—but not a contemporary beast, not something alive; a sort of archaeological artifact, a dark reconstructed skeleton of what the stadium would look like at some time far in the future: intact but lifeless. And what about the New-Sport of prosemaking in the far future? I thought then. Would that be preserved too? Or would it—and me and those like me—be long-lost in time, dead, gone, no longer even a memory?

These were dark thoughts and they made me even more uneasy than I already was because I didn't know where they'd come from, why all of a sudden I should be having such gloomy, even mystical visions. Maybe it was the tension, the constant pressure not just of the past few hours but of the past few months: the play-offs, Mort's rigorous training program, and now Huxtable's bribe attempt and threats and the kidnapping of my girl. Everything would be better once Sally was safe again and Huxtable and Rollo were in jail; once the Prose Bowl was over and the championship belonged to me.

Wouldn't it?

Sure it would. Of *course* it would.

I moved into the shadows near the escalator belts and let my eyes roam the empty tiers of seats, the field below. A pale light shone intermittently at the north end, but that would only be a security Servo making his desultory rounds. The stillness in this section remained absolute.

The cold was beginning to seep inside me now, numbing my legs and feet; I had to keep moving back and forth for blood circulation. The glowing numerals on my chronometer said it had been almost an hour since I'd left my apartment. Huxtable might have been calling from somewhere near the perimeter of the megalopolis, but even so, you could get almost anywhere in New York by express aircab within forty-five minutes. So why wasn't he here yet with Sally?

Unless he wasn't going to bring her at all, I thought. Unless he was planning some kind of trap to catch me too and wanted to make me sweat for a while before he sprang it.

The fear rose up again, seemed to clot in my throat so that I couldn't swallow. The only way I could fight off the urge to panic was to think about something else, occupy my mind with happy thoughts instead of the grim images that kept trying to form.

I forced myself to concentrate on New-Sport, the one thing I knew most about. In my mind's eye I replayed some of my own matches here in the Ultradome: the bitterly contested 28-word victory over Kate Day, The Kentucky Knuckler, in my very first pro face-off; the disappointing 60-word loss to Downbeat Dennis Dugan the following season, when I had a mental lapse and had to take a last-second fuschia-and-gold penalty flag for Murky Metaphor; the 1100-word scuff of the Quality Lit Kid, who drew Blazing Western Action in the first play-off match for both of us two seasons ago and kept taking penalties for having his Marshal mount cows instead of horses and kill villains with a five-shooter; my quarterfinal loss last year to The Hackensack Hack, who overtook me in the last quarter with his own special combination of exposition and shattering multiple plot twists. It seemed as though I could hear, standing there alone in the shadows, the ghostly echoes of all the cheers and all the boos; see the prose printout and the numerals flashing on the boards; feel the sweat and strain, the joy of victory and the agony of defeat.

And I thought, in spite of myself, of next Sunday and the Big Face-Off out in the Greater Los Angeles Coliseum. Even with Sally's life in jeopardy, maybe my own life too, I wondered how it would be down there on the floor of the Prose Bowl, with a hundred thousand fans surrounding me and fifty million more TriDim viewers hanging on my every move behind the machine, my every word flashing like spokes of fire on the giant boards.

It was strange, even scary, but a top-grade pulpeteer couldn't be touched or affected in the place from which the pulp came; Mort had told me that on almost the first day I'd met him, and I'd heard it from other pros since. And it was absolutely true. A prosemaker can produce in any circumstances; he can lose someone he cares about, have his personal life thrown into chaos, be cheated by unscrupulous agents or Editors, be hurt in all the ways any human can be hurt—pulpeteers are human too, Mort had once said—but all of it remained outside that part where the words were stroked and created to come pouring out through the fingertips and onto those giant shining boards. A man can be destroyed, the old twentieth-century pulpeteer Ernest Hemingway had written, but he cannot be defeated. Maybe that was inspirational and maybe it wasn't, but at this moment—

At this moment there was movement off to my left, the tall shadow of a man just slipping out of the C Section tunnel.

The muscles bunched up tight across my shoulders; my hand was suddenly slippery around the cold grip of the tranq weapon. I pressed back deeper into the shadows, drawing the weapon, holding it close to my body, and peered toward the man-shape to see if he was heading in my direction.

He was, at a slow and apparently aimless pace. One of the security Servos? Huxtable? Rollo? Well, I thought grimly, it won't be long before I find out. The figure was fifty meters away now and still coming.

I made a decision. He was alone and I was alone, and maybe I'd never get another chance like this one. The strategy was offense, not defense; I had to be the aggressor.

Forty meters.

I tensed even more, crouching.

Thirty meters.

My breath seemed to clog in my lungs; I opened my mouth wide to get enough air.

Twenty meters.

I raised the tranq weapon, thumbing off the safety mechanism. And took out my intraflash and held that ready too.

Ten meters.

I could see now that he had his hands in his coat pocket, that he wasn't wearing any headgear or a respirator, that he was about Huxtable's height and build. When he got just a little closer I ought to be able to recognize him. . . .

Five meters.

And I was so startled when I finally did see his face that I let out an involuntary gasp. It wasn't Huxtable at all. It wasn't anybody I had expected or even imagined I would encounter under these circumstances.

It was The Cranker.

3

The sound of my gasp froze him in position, his hands half out of his coat pockets. I jumped out in front of him, leveling both the tranq weapon and the infraflash, and snapped, "All right, Culp, don't try anything or you're sedated." Then I switched on the flash and shined it on his face.

His expression wasn't what I thought I'd see either; it was one of sheer astonishment. He said, "Is that you, Sackett? Rex Sackett?"

"You know damned well it's me," I said. "What are you doing here? Are you in with the kidnappers, is that it?"

"Kidnappers? What kidnappers?"

"Huxtable and that other bastard who snatched my girl Sally. You don't know anything about that, I suppose?"

"No," he said, "I don't. Is that why *you're* here? You're supposed to meet these kidnappers?"

"Yes." Confusion was starting to swirl inside me again; I didn't know what to think. "You're not one of them?"

"Hell, no," The Cranker said. "Listen, I'm sorry to hear about your girl; only swine would do a thing like that. What happened, kid?"

"I don't know if I should tell you. If you're not one of them, what are you doing here, walking around the Ultra-dome at night? I thought you were still out in Las Vegas."

"I came in on a superjet this afternoon," Culp said. "And

the reason I'm here is that it's where I always come after my matches." A sardonic smile curled the corners of his mouth. "It's the only place hacks like us have to come to. Or haven't you figured that out yet?"

I stared at him, remembering all the times I'd come to the Dome myself to relive my victories, and my losses too, when nobody else was around. "Well, I do stop by here sometimes, that's true," I admitted.

"I thought so. It's something almost all of us do, you know, but we don't talk about it—like we don't talk about a lot of things. The agents and Editors, the fans and the scribes, they've all done a pretty fair job of keeping us at a distance from each other, making us fear and distrust each other. But the fact is, kid"—the sardonic smile again—"we're all the same."

"The same?"

"Right out of the same mold," The Cranker said quietly. "If you've got any sensitivity at all, you'll find that out too someday."

My thoughts had stopped splintering; I had a grip on myself again. And a kind of relief moved through me: The Cranker *wasn't* in league with Huxtable and Rollo, I was convinced of that now; he was here for the reason he'd said he was. He was still the same honest pulpeteer I'd respected and idolized for so many years, still the Grand Old Man of New-Sport.

Still my opponent next Sunday in the Prose Bowl, I thought.

It gave me a sudden chill to realize that here we were, this season's Prose Bowl finalists, meeting together in a dark stadium just a few days before the Big Face-Off. It didn't seem right, somehow, even though it was accidental and there was nothing shady about it. The Cranker was the last man to stand between me and the championship; in a sense he was as much my enemy as Huxtable was. That was a cold hard fact, not something built up by agents and Editors and fans and scribes.

Culp was wrong about that. And he was wrong about all us prosemakers being the same, too. We weren't the same—we just weren't. How could he say we were all out of the same mold?

"You want to shut off that light now, kid?" The Cranker said. He was blinking at me, squinting. "It hurts my eyes."

I'd forgotten about the light. And what the light meant, too: not only was it hurting Culp's eyes, it could alert the security Servos that there were trespassers inside the Ultradome or Huxtable, if he was lurking somewhere nearby, that I wasn't alone as I was supposed to be. I shut off the infraflash, stowed it away inside my coat pocket, then peered around in all directions. But the darkness was unbroken everywhere. And so was the silence; the only sounds were the thin rasp of my breathing and the phlegmy wheeze of The Cranker's.

Culp stepped closer to me and I could smell the sharp odor of Fuel leaking out of him. "You want to talk about this kidnapping business?" he asked. "Get it off your chest?"

"No, I can't."

"It's got something to do with the Prose Bowl, I'll bet."

I stiffened. "How did you know that?"

"It didn't take any great mental effort," The Cranker said. "The girl of a top wordsmith gets snatched a few days before the Big Face-Off—what else would it involve? Gambling tie-in, probably. Somebody's after you to throw the match, right?"

"No," I said too quickly.

"Sure," Culp said. "Well, I'm not surprised. It's happened before."

"It has?"

"Of course it has. That's another thing nobody talks about."

"You mean past Prose Bowls have been *fixed*?"

"More or less. Everything connected with pulpeteering is fixed in one way or another."

"I don't believe that."

"Then you don't know much about the business."

"I know everything I need to know."

"You do, huh? What do you think of Jack Woodford?"

"Woodford? Who's he?"

"I thought so," The Cranker said. "He was a twentieth-century wordsmith, lived about a hundred years or so ago. Go look up some of his work, if you can find it; he'll tell you what prosemaking is all about."

"How can he?" I said. "If he lived a hundred years ago, that was long before New-Sport. What could he know about what it's like for us—what it's like for a pulpeteer?"

"Everything, kid," Culp said solemnly. "Woodford knew everything and he said it all."

I could feel myself growing more nervous and impatient as the seconds passed. I didn't want to hear about Jack Woodford or about past Prose Bowls being fixed; I didn't want to listen to The Cranker at all, or have him standing here next to me in the darkness. All I wanted was for Huxtable to bring Sally so I could see her and know she was all right and then try to find a way to save her.

I lifted my chronometer up close to my eyes and peered at its dial. The time now was 2220. Twenty minutes late, I thought. Why? Did The Cranker scare them off by showing up like he did? Is Huxtable just trying to make me sweat? *Why aren't they here?*

"You're pretty edgy, kid," Culp said. "How about a little shot of Fuel to soothe you out?"

"I don't want any Fuel."

"No? Every pulpeteer wants Fuel."

"I don't need it."

"That's what you think. Hell, Fuel is the secret and the answer; Fuel is the gospel according to Woodford. Pulpeteers have to have it because we feel and react more strongly than most citizens; that's why the government gives the best of us Unlimited Fuel cards. It's the only way we can keep our reactions from tearing us into little pieces. At least for awhile, anyhow."

Anger flared up inside me. Maybe The Cranker was

Fueled himself; maybe that was why he was saying all these crazy things. Or worse yet, much worse, I thought suddenly, maybe he was trying to capitalize on the kidnapping of Sally, on my emotional upheaval, for his own benefit.

I snapped, "Are you mind-psyching me, Cranker?"

"Mind-psyching?"

"That's right. You know I don't intend to throw the Prose Bowl, but you might think I can be psyched into it. Or at least psyched into losing my competitive edge. You'd like that either way, wouldn't you? Either way *you'd* win the championship."

There was silence for several seconds. Then Culp began to laugh—a low, terrible, mirthless sound. It went on for almost half a minute before trailing off into a series of soft hacking coughs. "Christ," he said when he'd caught his breath, "you think I want to win that badly? You think any of it matters that much to me?"

"Yes."

"Why? Because it matters that much to *you?*"

"Now listen, Cranker—"

"No, you listen. If you listened to what people had to say, you wouldn't be so goddamn naive. Or maybe it's just that you're plain dense. Don't you understand anything, kid? Doesn't anything ever penetrate and trigger an insight in that pulpeteer's brain of yours?"

"That's enough," I said, "that's all I'm going to take. You get away from me, old man; you're in the way, you're keeping me from saving my girl. That's all I'm thinking about right now, but when the Prose Bowl comes I'll be ready for you. You hear me? I'll be ready for you."

Another silence. Then Culp said, "Sure you will," in a funny kind of voice that seemed to have sadness and bitterness and disgust all mixed up in it. "You'll be ready for me."

"And I'll scuff you too," I said. "I'm thirty years younger than you and better than you ever were; it took you four decades to get to the Prose Bowl and it only took me six years."

"That's right," he said. In the darkness I saw his arm raise up in a profile silhouette as he took a long swallow from his container of Fuel. "Have it your own way."

"Go on, get away from me. Just . . . leave me alone."

"Sure, kid. But don't worry too much about your girl; you'll get her back all right. That part of it is fixed too. More or less. In one way or another."

You're crazy, I thought, but I didn't say it; he was already starting away, swaying a little from all the Fuel he'd had, toward the C Section tunnel. You're a crazy Fueled old man. They'll put you in an institution someday, Cranker, just like they did with Downbeat Dennis Dugan when he went berserk and tried to strangle the Head Editor in that Futuristic Fic League match last year.

But I hope they don't do it until after the Prose Bowl. I hope you last that long. Then I'll show you what's fixed and what isn't. Then I'll show you what pulpeteering is all about.

Then I'll show you.

I was shaking as I pressed back into the shadows. I took several deep breaths, with my eyes squeezed shut and my mouth open wide, and forced my mind to empty out all thoughts one by one, which was a trick I'd developed to use before a face-off; that helped me to get calm again. When I glanced over toward the C Section tunnel The Cranker was no longer in sight. Nobody was in sight and nothing moved anywhere, nothing made even the faintest sound.

Standing there, then, I felt as if I'd been swallowed up inside the huge black beast that was the Dome. And yet the beast was only a skeleton, with plenty of openings between its gigantic ribs. I could get out any time I wanted to. I could still get out.

Only I didn't, I *couldn't*. I waited instead, my fingers tight around the tranq weapon in my coat pocket.

And waited and kept on waiting.

Twenty-three hundred hours came and went. But not Huxtable and not my Sally.

They never came at all.

4

It was after midnight when I got back to my Complex. And for that matter I almost didn't get back at all. Staying out so late on the streets isn't safe, particularly in a deserted area like the one around the Ultradome; on my way to the aircab station two thuggers jumped me out of the snow-banked alley. It was a good thing I still had my tranq weapon in my pocket and that my hand was resting on it. I got it out in time and shot one of them just below the sternum and the other one in the vicinity of the carotid artery, and they both dropped like stones at my feet. Otherwise they would probably have got me—maybe even killed me by pouring poisoned Fuel down my throat, which is what some of the more ruthless thuggers were doing to their victims nowadays. And then what would have happened to Sally?

What *had* happened to Sally? And to Huxtable?

The question plagued me. There were a couple of possible answers, at least as far as I could see. One, Huxtable had brought Sally to the stadium and then either been scared off by the security Servos or warned off because he'd spotted me talking to The Cranker. Or two, he'd never intended to bring Sally from the beginning, but had come by himself and hidden somewhere to watch what I did, see if I followed orders—a kind of test of my obedience and also of my capitulation. I tried to tell myself that in any case I was sure to get another vi-com call tonight or early tomorrow, with further instructions. But that didn't reassure me very much.

The prospect of waiting out the rest of the night in my tomb-quiet apartment made me quiver inside. But I had to do it, and without Fuel too. Or at least, without too much Fuel. I *could* have a few ounces now, couldn't I? I was entitled to that much, wasn't I? Besides, I was numb with cold and still a little shaken by my experiences with The Cranker and the two thuggers.

I poured myself three ounces and drank it in quick sips. When it hit my stomach it seemed to set off a muffled little explosion that sent warmth flying outward in all directions like pieces of shrapnel. I began to soothe out right away—not much but just enough to take the edge off my anxiety. I'd told The Cranker that I didn't need the Fuel and that was true enough; I could take it or leave it alone. In a way, though, I had to admit he'd been right about us pulpeteers feeling and reacting more strongly than most citizens, about the Fuel helping to keep our reactions from tearing us up inside.

But I didn't want to think about The Cranker. Not until Sally was safe, anyway. Then I would think about him a lot and keep thinking about him until it was time to go out in the Prose Bowl on Sunday and scuff him like he'd never been scuffed before. Some of the crazy and insulting things he'd said tonight were lodged like bone splinters inside my mind; they'd irritate me for a long time.

Should I have another three ounces or so? I thought I could handle a full six ounces without risking a Fuel overload, so I went ahead and measured them out and sipped them down. These three ounces didn't explode; they just kind of glided and whispered through me, all soft and caressing.

Then the vi-com rang.

I ran over to it, switched on, and almost shouted hello. But it wasn't Huxtable. It was some damned scribe who was half-Fueled and who said he was calling "to get The Metaphor Kid's middle-of-the-night thoughts on what it's like to go up against a living legend called The Cranker." They have a way of asking questions like that, as if you're not a person but merely a piece of equipment; most scribes and New-Sport TriDim announcers seem to think pulpeteers are Servo-heads anyway, at least when we're not in competition, and talk to us as if we were. You can get used to it but not when your girl has been kidnapped and you're waiting for word from her abductors at 0100 hours in the morning; I told him a few things in language that surprised even me and then broke the connection. I could imagine him having the whole thing on tape and going to the Network in the morning and making a TriDim clip with some of the words cleaned out, which would be shown with commentary claiming it reflected how badly I was feeling the pressure. But I just didn't care.

I put on the TriDim to get rid of the rethickened silence. There wasn't anything on at this hour except repeats of the old Quality Lit Theater; the one tonight was another incomprehensible but kind of elegant play by that great old hack Will Shakespeare, called *King Lear*. I tried watching it for a while. It didn't make any sense to me, but then, Quality Lit isn't supposed to make sense. Or so Mort said to me once.

Before long, in spite of the tension, I began to feel drowsy—a combination of fatigue and the Fuel I'd just had and the TriDim images capering around me and muttering their arcane dialogue. I must have dozed off then. And slept quite a while, too, because the next thing I knew there was a faint light seeping through the windows and nothing at all on the TriDim except flickering grayness.

I sat up, blinking and rubbing my gritty eyes; my mouth was dry and I had a thin pulsing headache. I looked at my chronometer. 0645 hours. Almost dawn.

And Huxtable still hasn't called, I thought. Why not? What's he waiting for?

Sally, I thought. If he's done anything to her, if he's hurt her or *touched* her and made her impure, I'll tear his leg off and beat him to death with it. I will, too. That's a promise.

When I stood up my eye fell on the Fuel container. It

seemed to wink back at me in a sort of seductive way. I forced myself to ignore it; it was too early for my first narrative hook of the day. Instead I went to the Nutritional Unit and dialed a vita-breakfast and a cup of real-coffee. Then I took both to the window and stared out at the dawn breaking through a high mist—no snow today and maybe just a hint of cold sunlit blue far off to the east.

The megalopolis was just stirring into wakefulness. Some of the windows in the other Sky Complexes turned into lighted rectangles as I watched, and aircabs and early commuter airtrams were visible high above. At one of the nearby Complexes a team of Informational technicians, like the one Dad works on, was building a new sign up around the 200th floor. I could hear the noise of their tools filtering in through the plastoid.

I watched the technicians for a time, drinking my vita-breakfast and my coffee. When I was done with both I went back to the couch and sat looking blankly at the flickering TriDim screen. Something began to tickle the back of my mind, in a way that made me frown. I took out the Special Pass card I'd found in Sally's apartment and stared at it for several seconds, letting my thoughts drift this way and that, back over everything that had happened since Sunday and my victory over the Kansas City Flash.

And pretty soon certain little facts began to connect and interlock with other little facts, so that a hazy pattern took shape. Like a Blazing Western Action or Futuristic Fic plot does when you're in the first few hundred words of a face-off and everything is just beginning to mesh in that place where the prose comes from.

But this wasn't a prose plot forming inside me now; it was a *real* plot, an ugly plot that made me gasp when I saw it clearly for the first time. A chill ran up and down my back. Then I had a hot flash that made my ears burn. Then I was sick to my stomach and I had to jump up and run into the bathroom cubicle, getting to the saniflush just in time to keep from throwing up my vita-breakfast all over the floor.

I didn't feel any less sick after that. As I let the Brusher scrub my teeth I tried to tell myself that I was imagining things; but I knew I wasn't. It all interlocked too solidly, made too much sense, to be anything except the truth—the most terrible truth I had ever had to face.

The vi-com rang again as I was coming out of the bathroom.

I didn't lunge for it as I had the other times; instead I just walked over to it and switched on in a sort of numb machinelike way. I knew it would be Huxtable on the other end. And it was.

"Still being a good little boy, Sackett?" his voice said. The screen stayed dark, as it had the first time he'd called last night; and more noise came over the wire, too, just like the first time.

"Yes," I said.

"I thought you might be. I saw you at the stadium, you know; I even listened to you talking to The Cranker."

"Then why didn't you meet with me like you promised?"

He made a low chuckling sound. "I'm one of the bad guys, remember?" he said. "I don't have to keep my promises unless I feel like it."

"You were just testing me, weren't you?"

"That's it, kid. And you get a passing grade. So far."

"I want to talk to Sally," I said.

"Not just yet."

"Is she all right? Damn you, you haven't hurt her—"

"She's just fine. All snug and cozy."

"When can I see her?"

"Pretty soon," Huxtable said. "When we're sure you'll do exactly what you're told to do in the Prose Bowl."

"I will," I lied. "I'll do whatever you want."

"Just keep saying that to yourself, kid. While you sit there in your nice little apartment and wait for me to call again."

The vi-com went silent.

I switched off and stood there shaking. Rage was boiling

up inside me now, a really outraged rage, because there was no more doubt in my mind that I knew the truth, the whole truth, and nothing but the truth.

I knew where Huxtable was.

I knew where Sally was.

I knew *everything*.

But what was I going to do about it? The logical thing was to go to the authorities, let them take over. Only the police were just another bureaucratic agency, filled with levels of deceit and incompetence; it would probably take me hours to convince someone to listen to my story and double that to get them to believe it and do something about it.

The hell with the police, I thought and went over and checked my tranq weapon. I don't need the damn police, I thought and threw on my coat. They're just a bunch of Servos anyway.

Saving Sally was up to Rex Sackett, The Metaphor Kid— only not a *kid* at all, not anymore, as I would show a lot of people pretty quick.

Saving Sally was up to *me*.

5

The Sky Complex was one of those fancy new ones along the filled-in line of what had once been the Harlem River: luminescent pink facade, replete with the newest in color-bright Informationals and an ultramodern rooftop aircab station. Behind it, on the fill-land, another Complex was under construction. That one was ablaze with the infralights of nightworkers and Servo helpers, and you could hear the heavy rumbling purr of machinery.

When I left the aircab and approached the Checkpoint I pulled up the collar of my coat and ducked my head down into it, so that the lower half of my face was hidden. I had the Special pass card in my right hand and I walked in a sort of hard, clipped stride. That was how government agents looked and acted—the ones I'd seen on TriDim, at least. My impersonation ought to be good enough to fool the Checkpoint Servo, particularly when I showed him the Special card. They're almost never questioned.

The Servo watched me come up to him, peered at my face, and said, "Wow, you're Rex Sackett, you're The Metaphor Kid."

Damn! "Oh," I said, "you recognized me."

"Sure thing, Mr. Sackett. A famous prosemaker like you? Wow. Will you give me your autograph? My wife would love to have it; she thinks you're terrific. So do I, but she's really one of your biggest fans."

I mumbled something gracious and fumbled out my Smoothwriter. As I signed the notepad the Servo handed me I tried to figure a way to get inside without going through procedure and without the Special card. But there wasn't one that I could see. The only thing I could do was to show the Special and say that I'd gotten it from a government agent and was here on a secret assignment.

"Thanks a lot, Mr. Sackett," the Servo said when I gave him back the pad. "You can go on in now."

"Uh, I can?"

"Sure thing." He winked at me. "No need to bother with security; I know who *you* are, don't I."

"Yes," I said, "right, you do."

"Want me to announce you?"

"Uh, no. I'll just, uh, go right up."

"Sure thing, Mr. Sackett."

I hurried in past him and into the chute. That was simple, I thought; I never expected it would be that simple. And then, for no good reason, I remembered something The Cranker had said last night at the Ultradome: *"Don't worry too much about your girl; you'll get her back all right. That part of it is fixed too. More or less. In one way or another."* Just crazy talk. And yet . . .

No, just crazy talk. How could it be anything else? The Cranker didn't know what he was saying about a lot of things that had to do with pulpeteering. Maybe we didn't matter much to New-Sport media types like Harmon Penn, which was what I'd come to think, but we did matter to the fans like the Checkpoint Servo and his wife. We *mattered*, that was all there was to it. Of course we did.

The chute deposited me on the 500th floor, near the top, and I turned left down the corridor to the door with the numerals 50016 etched on it. There was nobody else in sight. I took out my tranq weapon as I went and carried it down low along my right leg, my finger tight against the release mechanism, the safety off.

When I reached the door I stopped alongside it and flattened myself against the wall so that I couldn't be seen through the scanner inside. I could feel myself shaking internally, all of the rage pouring in from the edges and centering in my throat; I took several deep breaths to keep myself calm and avoid the danger of hyperventilation. This isn't much different than a face-off, I kept reminding myself; it takes the same kind of will, the same kind of iron nerve, the same kind of coolness and poise under pressure.

With my left hand I eased the Special pass card a half inch into the slot above the computer-lock in the door. But then I held it poised there, with still another half inch to go before it activated the computer and unlocked the door. I was about as positive as I could be that Huxtable was in there, that Sally was in there, but I had to know for certain before I made my move. Also, I wanted Huxtable—or Rollo, either one—close to the door so I'd know exactly where at least one of them was and maybe be able to catch him off-guard when I went in.

Then I held my breath and passed my hand through the light beam for the door chimes.

Nothing happened for about ten seconds. My heart was pelting away in my chest and I had to dry my palm and fingers because they sweat-slicked the grip of the tranq weapon. The moment of reckoning was only an instant or two away—

Footsteps sounded faintly. And then the scanner eye opened and the scan-com made its usual crackling sound. Huxtable's voice, metallic but recognizable, said, "Who is it?"

That was when I moved. I let the trapped air come spewing out between my teeth, jammed the Special card all the way into the slot, threw my shoulder against the door just as the computer-lock clicked and released.

And the same thing happened inside my mind that had happened in Sally's apartment yesterday: nightmarish surreality, everything reduced to a kind of terrible slow motion in which I was both participant and pulpeteer omniscient—a scene from one of my face-offs translated into tense, real-life terms. . . .

THE DOOR SLAMMED INWARD AGAINST A

YIELDING BODY AND SACKETT HEARD A STARTLED YELP OF PAIN AS HUXTABLE WAS DRIVEN BACK- WARD AND THROWN TO THE FLOOR. THEN THE DE- TERMINED YOUNG PROSEMAKER WAS INSIDE THE DIMLY LIT BUT SUMPTUOUSLY FURNISHED APART- MENT, HIS STEELY EYES SEARCHING THE ROOM WITH EAGER ANTICIPATION. HE DIDN'T SEE SALLY BUT HE DID SEE ROLLO JUST EMERGING FROM A SECOND ROOM.

ROLLO HAD AN OLD-FASHIONED .45 IN ONE CLAWLIKE FIST; HE DUCKED TO ONE SIDE, INTO A CROUCH, AND SENT A BUZZING SLUG PAST SACK- ETT'S RIGHT EAR. IT DIDN'T FAZE THE COURA- GEOUS PULPETEER. CALMLY HE TRIGGERED HIS OWN WEAPON, SAW THE TRANQ DART STRIKE HOME IN ROLLO'S FLABBY NECK. ROLLO DROPPED HIS ROD AND PITCHED FORWARD ON HIS FACE WITHIN SECONDS AS THE DOUBLE DOSE OF SEDA- TIVE COURSED THROUGH HIS BLOODSTREAM AND NUMBED HIS CORRUPT BRAIN.

HUXTABLE WAS ON HIS FEET BY THIS TIME, JUST STARTING TO CHARGE SACKETT. THE VALIANT WORDSMITH FIRED AGAIN, BUT IN HIS HASTE HIS SHOT WAS WIDE AND DID NOTHING BUT GOUGE SPLINTERS OUT OF ONE WALL. THEN HUXTABLE WAS ON HIM AND THE TWO MEN STRUGGLED, A GRIM AND MORTAL STRUGGLE THAT TOOK THEM CRASHING AND STAGGERING AROUND THE ROOM, UPSETTING FURNITURE, CAROMING OFF THE WALLS. HUXTABLE CURSED STEADILY, ADDING VILE EPITHETS TO THE THUNDEROUS NOISE, AND ALSO BREATHED TERRIBLE FUMES INTO SACKETT'S FACE AS HE SOUGHT TO DESTROY THE INTREPID YOUNG HACK'S MANHOOD WITH AN UPTHRUST KNEE, SOUGHT TO WRENCH THE TRANQ WEAPON INTO HIS OWN VENAL GRASP.

BUT SACKETT CLUNG GRIMLY TO THE WEAPON,

116

TRYING TO TURN IT TOWARD HUXTABLE INSTEAD. THEN THE TWO COMBATANTS TRIPPED AS ONE OVER A FREE-FORM SCULPTURE OF AN OBSCURE OLD-SPORT BASEBALL PLAYER NAMED BABE RUTH, AND WHEN THEY THUDDED TO THE FLOOR SACK-ETT MANAGED TO SPRAWL HALF ON TOP OF THE WRETCHED FELON. THE BREATH WAS MOMENTAR-ILY KNOCKED OUT OF HUXTABLE: FOR AN INSTANT HE LAY MOTIONLESS, GASPING. THIS GAVE SACKETT TIME TO WEDGE THE TRANQ WEAPON BETWEEN THEIR HEAVING BODIES.

HE PULLED THE TRIGGER.

THE DART PENETRATED HUXTABLE'S FLESH JUST BELOW THE THIRD RIB AND SENT PARALYZING FLUID STRAIGHT INTO HIS VITALS.

THE WICKED EX-EDITOR GRUNTED, THRASHED ABOUT FOR A FEW SECONDS. HIS BREATH BELCHED OUT THEN IN A LONG SIGH, HIS EYES GLAZED, AND HE WAS STILL.

THE BATTLE WAS OVER.

AND THIS TIME IT WAS REX SACKETT WHO WAS THE VICTOR AND THE VILLAINS WHO WERE DOWN AND OUT.

I got up on shaky legs and stood panting over Huxtable, feeling weak but elated. The surreality was gone now; it was as if I had just awakened from a desperate dream. I sensed that the omniscient literary quality of the fight had made the difference, given me the edge I'd needed to overwhelm the two kidnappers. In the world of prose, good always triumphs over evil: The pulpeteer *knows* as he's cranking how an ulti-mate confrontation like this one must and will turn out. The hero can't lose, he's invincible. I had written myself as the hero; I was invincible.

But I didn't have time to dwell on that sort of abstract thinking. Now that I'd vanquished Huxtable and Rollo, Sally's welfare was uppermost in my mind. I stepped over the two fallen bodies and hurried across to the doorway to the apartment's second room. When I stepped through it I saw it had a decadent circular bed and that the walls and ceiling were all mirrors made out of real glass. My heart skipped a beat; the mirrors reflected a dozen Rex Sacketts, a dozen expressions of horrified concern.

Sally was lying in the middle of the bed, fully clothed but bound and gagged cruelly. And one corner of her tunic was torn, revealing a patch of soft white flesh!

I rushed to her, murmuring her name, and fumbled and tore at her bonds to set her free. Her eyes stared up at me with a mixture of relief and brimming emotion. When I finally got her hands untied and the gag stripped away from her mouth, she threw her arms around me and cried, "Oh, Rex, you've saved me! You've saved me!"

"Are you all right?" I asked, holding her.

"Yes. Yes."

"I mean"—and I swallowed heavily; the words were almost too awful to speak aloud—"I mean, they didn't . . . do anything to you, did they? They didn't . . . *soil* you?"

She blushed. "Oh, no, nothing like that happened."

"But your tunic is torn—"

"It ripped when that one beast pushed me inside the porto-carrier yesterday," Sally said. She lowered her eyes. "I'm . . . still the same for you, Rex."

"Thank God," I said.

And once more, like an echo at the back of my mind, I heard The Cranker's voice saying, *"Don't worry too much about your girl; you'll get her back all right. That part of it is fixed too. More or less. In one way or another . . ."*

I shook my head hard and the echo faded. Sally was saying, "But how did you find me, Rex? How did you know this was where they'd taken me?"

"It's a long story," I said. "I'll explain it to you later, after we've gotten out of here."

"Rex, you know who's behind this whole terrible thing."

The anger burned inside me again, like an old-fashioned wood fire that had just had a fresh log dumped on it. "I know," I said. I helped her to her feet, put my arm around her, and we started out of that awful room. "And I'm going to tell the authorities—"

"You're not going to tell the authorities anything," a new voice said coldly. "Not a damned thing, Sackett."

I jerked my head up, staring; Sally cried out and clutched at me in fright. There were two men standing just inside the open entrance door to the apartment, and the one who had spoken was pointing a tranq weapon at Sally and me. I wasn't surprised to see the second man, the one with the sad and nervous look on his face, because this was his apartment. But I *was* surprised to see the one with the weapon—amazed to see him because I'd never suspected he was part of this criminal conspiracy to fix the Prose Bowl.

The second man was Mort Morgandahl, my once-trusted agent.

The man with the weapon was Harmon Penn.

6

Penn said to Mort, "Close the door, Morgandahl, we don't want your neighbors to hear any of this." But Mort didn't seem to hear him; he just stood there looking unhappy. So Penn had to close the door himself.

"Hello, kid," Mort said to me, soft-voiced. His eyes were distant and he wouldn't look at me squarely; his gaze flitted here and there in the room. "You really tore the place up, didn't you? Not to mention Huxtable and Rollo."

Penn made a snorting noise and his face had the same disgusted expression that it did most of the time on TriDim. "Our boy Sackett is a real hero," he said in his nasty way. "Aren't you, Sackett?"

But I ignored Penn. "Why?" I asked Mort. "Why did you do it? You were on top, Mort; you were a top agent with a pulpeteer in the Prose Bowl. Why did you have to go and destroy it all?"

"The Prose Bowl," he said remotely. "You know something, kid? I figured you had a shot to go all the way the first time I saw you write in competition. You were raw but you had energy, you had terrific drive, and you didn't depend on the adjectives the way so many beginners do. This kid could be my first Prose Bowl champion, I said to myself. I always wanted to handle a Prose Bowl champion."

"Then why, Mort? Why?"

"I needed the money," he said, "that's why."

"We all need the money," Penn said. "Everybody needs the old money. But now things have gotten complicated."

I said to Mort, "But I thought you had plenty of money: this fancy apartment, your suite of offices, the nice clothes you always wear. . . ."

"All of that's a front, kid," he said. "I've had client losses, gambling losses, personal problems. About six months ago I dropped a bundle to this syndicate up at Luna Colony and I couldn't pay off my markers. They sent Rollo around to talk to me a few weeks ago, when it began to look like you had a chance to go all the way. I didn't want to do what they asked but I didn't have any choice; I didn't want to end up like Wee-Wristed Wally Gold."

"Wee-Wristed Wally? What does he have to do with it?"

"You don't think he really broke both his legs in an accident up on Luna, do you?"

"You mean he didn't?"

"Hell, no. The fix was in last year too, only Wally couldn't go through with it and won the Face-Off instead. His payoff for that was a year in traction."

I felt a little sick to my stomach. The Cranker had been right about past Prose Bowls being fixed . . . and what if he'd been right in all the rest of things he'd said, too?

Sally clutched my arm and whispered, "I told you it was a terrible business, Rex. Didn't I tell you?"

Penn said, "Shut up, all of you. I need time to think."

I swallowed hard and said to Mort, "I can understand you trying to get me to throw the Prose Bowl, but how could you do it by using Sally? How could you be a party to her kidnapping?"

He swallowed too. "That part of it wasn't my idea, believe me. It was Penn and Huxtable who cooked it up."

"I'll cook *you*, Morgandahl," Penn said, "if you don't shut up."

"I tried to talk them out of it," Mort said to me, "but they said it was the only way you could be pushed into losing the match on Sunday."

"Losing it?" I said. "You mean throwing it."

"Either way. The idea all along was to psych you into losing your competitive edge, get you so strung out you wouldn't know what you were doing out there in the Coliseum; that's why Penn came down on you so hard in the postgame interview last Sunday. If you agreed to throw the match, fine; but if you didn't, you'd lose anyway because of the pressure."

Psyched into losing my competitive edge. That was what I'd accused The Cranker of trying to do at the Ultradome last night. And all along it had been Mort. . . .

"But you weren't bending far enough to suit the great Penn," Mort said. "He wanted to put more pressure on you and that's where the kidnapping came in."

"I'll put pressure on your head if you don't shut up," Penn said.

None of us even looked at him. Penn's threats, I had come to realize, were something like his commentaries on TriDim: They had form but no substance. Just as his commentaries seemed to be insights but were simply words and quasi-authoritative ramblings, so his threats were his idea of what *ought* to scare a pulpeteer. And maybe I wasn't the only person who understood this about him, either. I remembered Ralph, the Fueltender in my Complex, telling me about the rumor that Penn's TriDim popularity was fading and he was due to be replaced. That could be the real reason why Penn was involved in this gambling-and-bribery scheme.

"We all underestimated you, kid," Mort said to me. "Me most of all. You know what I told them when they first approached me? I told them you were so stupid and trusting that I could handle you with no problem, that you'd never figure out what was going on."

"Did you really believe that?"

"I guess I did, kid."

"I'm not a kid," I said. "And I'm not stupid, either. I figured out what was going on, all right; I figured it out pretty fast once I put my mind to it."

"So you did. How? Was it something I said?"

"No. But part of it was something you did."

"I've heard just about enough from all of you," Penn said. "Listen here, Morgandahl, we've got to figure out what to do with Sackett and the girl. I think we might be able to make it look like a suicide pact. All we have to do is get one of them to write a note."

Mort said to me, "What was it that I did?"

"You've got a habit of pulling something out of your coat pocket—usually a Complex pass card—when you're angry and waving it in a person's face. You did it on TriDim after the semifinal match, when Penn and Vinnie Winkle were interviewing us, and you did it again in your office yesterday when Diana made a remark to you. In your office the card you pulled out was pink, which made it your pass card because this Complex is pink. But on TriDim the card was whitish, the color of a Special pass card."

"And you wondered what I was doing with one of those."

"Not right then. Not even when I found a Special card in Sally's apartment, after Huxtable and Rollo abducted her and knocked me out. But later I made the connection: You gave the Special card to Huxtable so he could get into Sally's building without any problem; and so he could get into your Complex too, probably."

"Come to think of it," Penn said, "maybe an accident would be better. It shouldn't be too hard to make it look like a tragic accident of some kind."

"How did you know Sally was here?" Mort asked me. "The Special card couldn't have told you that, at least not conclusively."

"No, it was the background noise on the vi-com."

"Background noise?"

"When I called you Sunday night, after Huxtable first approached me in the Fuel lounge, I could hear construction noises in the background, from that new Complex that's going up next door to here. The same sort of noises were there both times when Huxtable called me too. The first time I thought it was just interference on the line; it wasn't until he called the second time, this morning, that I was positive of what it really was."

Sally looked up at me with shining eyes. "You are smart, Rex," she murmured. "Oh, you *are.*"

"A smart-*ass* is what he is," Penn growled. "But pretty soon he's going to be a dead-ass."

I said to Mort, "Diana gave me another clue too. I called your office after the kidnapping, because I wasn't thinking too clearly, and she said that maybe you hadn't left New York after all, that maybe your ticket was actually for today. Why would you tell me you were leaving yesterday if you were really leaving today? The only possible reason was that you didn't want me to know you were still in New York and maybe drop by your Complex and accidentally find out it was where Sally was."

"Goddamn it!" Penn shouted. "What's the matter with you people? Why won't you pay attention to me?"

"That Diana," Mort said, shaking his head. "She's vindictive, that's what she is; one little failure to perform and she violates her sacred oath of silence as an agent's secretary."

"Failure to perform what?" Sally asked.

"Never mind. Well, it doesn't matter, I guess. Diana didn't bring it all crashing down around my ears; neither did you, kid, for that matter. I did it to myself."

"I'm going to shoot all of you!" Penn screamed. He was dancing up and down now, waving his tranq weapon; his face was apoplectic and he was starting to drool on himself. "I'm going to shoot all of you if you don't listen to me! Triple suicide pact! Three-way accident! Shoot you all!"

"Oh, for Christ's sake, Harmon," Mort said, "you're not going to shoot anybody and you know it."

And he reached out and plucked the tranq weapon out of Penn's fingers.

Penn stopped dancing around and stared at Mort in wide-eyed disbelief. A funny sort of gurgling sound came out of him.

"It's all over," Mort said to him. "We're crooks and scoundrels, sure, but we're not murderers. We can't kill Rex and Sally; you know that as well as I do, you big Servo-head."

Penn gurgled again, wheeled around, ran to the door, threw it open, stumbled out, and disappeared in the direction of the chute.

I took a belated step forward, but Mort shook his head at me. "Let him go, kid. Where's he going to go anyway? He doesn't have any place to go."

I stood still again. Mort handed me the tranq weapon butt first and said, "I don't have any place to go either, but I guess I ought to try the same as Penn. If you're a crook and a scoundrel, you're supposed to make an effort to get away; it's a sort of code of the underworld. How about it, Rex? You can take me in if you want, and you don't owe me a damn thing, but I'd really appreciate maybe an hour's lead time."

"What will you do?"

He shrugged. "Maybe go out to Greater L.A. Maybe try to smuggle myself on a ship to Luna. Does it matter? They'll get me in the end; they always get us in the end."

I felt numb now; all the excitement, all the anger, all the pain had left me absolutely drained. I said, "All right, Mort," in a dull voice, and Sally's hand was tight and cold in mine as we moved forward, past Mort and the still-unconscious bodies of Huxtable and Rollo, not looking at Mort anymore, and out into the corridor. When we stepped into the chute a few seconds later I wondered if I'd ever see him—or Harmon Penn—again.

All the way down I hoped I never would.

7

Sally and the folks and I left for Greater Los Angeles as scheduled on Thursday morning, the day after Year Day. The hour-long flight seemed interminable, even though Sally and I held hands the whole time and all of us tried to talk about pleasant and uneventful things, like which was the best new Informational Dad's agency had put up for the holiday season.

There hadn't been a word on TriDim or in the sheets about Penn, Mort, Huxtable, or Rollo; I'd asked the authorities to keep the whole ugly scandal under wraps until after the Prose Bowl, and they'd agreed and surprised all of us by keeping their promise. If they'd arrested Mort or Penn or any of the others, I hadn't heard about it. And I didn't *want* to hear about it. All I wanted was to forget them and the things they'd done and tried to do to me and to Sally.

But if that was possible at all, it wasn't going to be easy. For one thing the story would break eventually, later if not sooner. The "official" line on Penn was that he'd suffered a mild heart attack and was in seclusion, obviously unable to take his usual place in the TriDim broadcast booth at the Prose Bowl. But the lie was pretty transparent and wouldn't hold up very long. As for Mort, I had already decided to explain his absence by issuing a simple statement that he was no longer my agent, for personal reasons, and refusing to comment further. That explanation wouldn't stand up long either; if anything, it would pique the media's interest and send them out sniffing around like a bunch of Servos after a regular job.

Then there was the ambivalence that kept swirling around inside me and wouldn't let me get my feelings sorted out about the business. I kept remembering that The Cranker had told me about past Prose Bowls being fixed, about all of pulpeteering being fixed in one way or another, and how all of us prosemakers were the same and none of us really mattered. I didn't want to believe any of those things, yet I couldn't disbelieve them either, not anymore. Being a wordsmith was my whole life; I had worked for years and years to get to the Prose Bowl and now I stood on the next to last plateau, with the ultimate prize just one short jump away. Only I couldn't seem to decide if all the leaping from one plateau to another, never thinking, just leaping like a mountain goat, had been and still was worth the effort.

Sally didn't think so, that was for sure. Every chance she had when we were alone together, she tried harder than ever to convince me New-Sport was ruining my life, that I owed it to myself and to her to quit after the Prose Bowl and move to Luna Colony or somewhere else as soon as we were married. "You've got to open your eyes, Rex," she said once. "You've got to look past the glitter of money and prestige and see what pulpeteering really is. You've had a glimpse these past few days, with Mort and Harmon Penn and all the rest; now you've got to really *look* at the business. Then you'll know that I'm right. Then you'll know your only hope is to get out before it's too late."

And maybe she was right, too.

But maybe she wasn't. . . .

The Greater L.A. skyport was jammed with fans and Tri-Dim cameras and media people when we finally landed. I forced myself to smile and answer questions, saying I was confident I could win on Sunday, even though The Cranker was a masterful prosemaker and I was honored just to be competing against him. I said a lot of other things too, about strategy and categories and other aspects of wordsmithing, but the truth was, I had been neglecting the mechanics of my game. No matter how I was feeling inside, I told myself as we piled into one of the special aircabs provided by the League Editors, I was going to have to knuckle down to basics immediately. Otherwise, that wily old Culp was liable to scuff me right out of the Coliseum—and the irony of that would be bitter, because it was just what Mort and Huxtable and Penn had intended in the first place.

The aircab took us to the Henry Kissinger Memorial Hotel and we checked in without being bothered too much more by the scribes and other media. Sally and I had separate rooms, of course, and the folks had a room just down the hall from us. I don't like to admit it, but the prospect of Sally and me being so close together for the next few days put some prurient thoughts into my head. If we hadn't had our pact to go to our marital bed pure and untouched, I guess I might have suggested something to her; the nights had been awfully long lately and it would have been good to have her help me get through the rest of them until Sunday. It couldn't be, though, so there was just no use in thinking about it. And at least I had the consoling thought that Huxtable and those other swine hadn't violated her when they had her defenseless in Mort's apartment.

On Friday morning there was a joint press conference for The Cranker and me at one of the Hollywood TriDim studios. Culp said nice things about me and I said the same about him, neither of us saying very much at all. When the conference was over, just before the media converged on us from all sides, The Cranker leaned over and whispered, "I see you got your girl back. I'm glad everything worked out, kid."

I looked at him and realized I didn't hate him anymore, or at least not in the volatile personal sense I'd hated him that night in the Ultradome. I wasn't so sure anymore that he was crazy, either; he looked sane enough, if a little weary and bloody-eyed from too much Fuel. I didn't know how I felt toward him, exactly. Maybe I didn't feel anything toward him; maybe I didn't *want* to feel anything toward him.

I said, "Thanks, Cranker. You were right when you said it

would." I started to ask him then what he'd meant the other night about it being fixed, too, that I would get Sally back unharmed, but his next words jarred the thought right out of my head.

"I can guess who was behind the kidnapping and gambling set-up," he said. His voice dropped even lower. "Your agent, right?"

"How did you know that?" I asked, amazed.

"I heard your statement about why Morgandahl's not here," The Cranker said. "Besides, I know all about New-Sport agents. Why do you think I don't have one myself any more?"

Before I could say anything to that, the scribes were all over us and we were pulled away from each other. And I knew the next time I saw him in person would be in the Prose Bowl.

I spent the rest of Friday and all day Saturday alone in my hotel room, practicing narrative hooks for the different categories, working out a game plan. Always before I'd had Mort to help me with my strategy and now it was up to me alone; I was pretty tentative at first, and it took me awhile, but I was proud of the way I eventually got things planned out. Sally and the folks spent both days sightseeing by aircab from one end of Greater L.A. to the other, hopping from town to town along the chain of them that stretched between the Mexican border and the wall of Sky Complexes that covered the Big Sur seacoast. Sally bought some souvenirs, mostly musical stuff, and Dad thought up three new Informationals that he said would earn him a promotion once he got back to New York and his agency. Nobody asked me how my practicing had gone.

Late Saturday afternoon I got a call from an Assistant League Editor named Urquhart, who at one time had been known as The Spaced-Out Spacer, a real Futuristic Fic whiz before he'd decided to enter business school and go into the management side of New-Sport. He told me that Penn and Mort and Huxtable and Rollo were all in custody. Penn, it seemed, had gone to the authorities of his own volition and tried to make a deal with them: He would turn in the others in exchange for the privilege of announcing the full story on TriDim on Prose Bowl eve.

"But they won't let him do that, will they?" I asked.

"No, of course not," Urquhart said. "The other three were rounded up not long after Penn showed, and besides, he's a psycho-schizoid; they had him examined yesterday, when he threw some kind of fit in custody, and now they've got him on sedatives." He sighed. "It's too bad this whole mess had to happen."

"That's for sure."

"Gives all of New-Sport a black eye, whether it's made public or not. But then, I guess we'll weather the storm—I guess we'll survive."

"Yes," I said. "We'll survive."

And then it was Sunday.

And then it was the Prose Bowl.

PART THREE

Prose Bowl

1

I had seen the Coliseum, the famed Prose Bowl, dozens of times on TriDim, but it was only two hours before the Big Face-Off that I finally saw it for real. It was an ancient and crumbling ruin, with massive age- and vandal-scars, art-deco paintings in poor taste, filthy scrawls of graffitti on its facade that gave it a scabrous and unwholesome appearance. I had the thought that on a bleak night, when there weren't thousands of fans streaming into it and no multicolored pennants and Informationals fluttered and blazed around its open-air rim, it would seem even more of an archaeological artifact than the New York Ultradome; that it would ripple and murmur with the ghosts of long-gone Old-Sport and New-Sport matches alike, long-dead pros who had had their moments of glory or minutes of agony within its walls.

Sally, the folks, and I arrived there from the hotel in a special aircab convoy. Mom and Dad were wearing proud smiles and were so excited that all they could do was to beam at me; but I knew they didn't really understand what had happened or what I was going to go through next. Sally held my hand and said almost nothing. She—and Mom, too—was wearing a Sackett Booster sweater with the big red S on the front and the red cuffs, and she looked very pretty and young. But I could still see hints of sadness in her face and doubt in her eyes.

We entered the Coliseum through the Competitors Entrance. The media people were held back by Servo lines, as were spectators who wanted close-up glimpses of the celebrity contestants. I heard all of them shouting and chattering, but I just looked straight ahead and kept silent, although I did wave my arms a few times.

Inside we were met by two Prose Bowl officials and several security Servos. The amenities were brief, and once they were over it was time for me to head for my locker room—I had been given the visitor's designation for the match, I was told—and for Sally and the folks to head for their special box seats in G Section, where the Sackett Boosters would be located. Dad shook my hand hard and wished me luck, and Mom cried and hugged me, and Sally kissed me on the mouth and whispered that she loved me. Then they were gone. And even though there were Servos and officials around, I felt that I was alone.

My locker room turned out to be huge and comfortable, complete not only with a deluxe Body-Ease and other equipment but with a private TriDim. It also had the familiar writer's-office odors of sweat, stale tobacco, and spilled Fuel, which assailed me and made me feel a little better. The Prose Bowl people were careful about creating the proper atmosphere, I knew; they wanted each of the contestants to feel as much at home as possible.

Just after I entered, the Servos who would be my Seconds out on the field arrived to introduce themselves. One of them handed me a Fuel container; I had a short three ounces and that made me feel better too, soothed me out a little. As soon as the Servos left, the Head Editor and the Line Editor came in for a short pro-forma discussion of the rules. I was glad when they were finally gone and I was truly alone for the first time. Preparing mentally for a match was the same as writing one, the same as almost every other aspect of prosemaking: you had to do it by yourself.

I undressed and spent fifteen minutes in the Body-Ease. My hamstring pull hadn't given me any trouble all week, but I thought that a pre-game massage would help keep it from stiffening up once the contest was underway. When I came out I put on my uniform jersey—the visitor's red—and then switched on the TriDim to have some sound and movement around me while I did my warm-up exercises.

The bands were out on the field now, marching and playing the kind of music that always stirs the blood before a face-off. And the New-Sport announcers were offering analyses of The Cranker's and my styles and approaches to a match, asking each other if the increased wordage per quarter—2500 words instead of the usual 2000—would work in my favor or in Culp's (mine, both of them agreed, because of my youth and stamina). The anchor man was Vinnie Winkle; the color commentator, filling in for Penn, was Lloyd Sheldrake. Once I heard them mention Penn's supposed heart attack, expressing sadness about it, but when I glanced up I saw that neither of them looked very sad at all. They looked pretty damned pleased, in fact, underneath their assumed expressions of sorrow.

As I was finishing my exercises, the TriDim cameras homed in on one of the scoreboards to show the time: it was only forty-five minutes until the match was scheduled to start.

Forty-five minutes, I thought. Forty-five minutes until The Cranker and I sit down across the Line from each other to find out which of us is the best pulpeteer in the world. Forty-five minutes until my lifelong dream becomes a reality, until I start firing out my prose in the greatest spectacle of them all.

And in spite of myself, in spite of everything, I felt a rising sense of excitement. The band music, the pageantry, the reverent voices of the TriDim announcers, the fan-swollen stands, the machines waiting silent and powerful at center field—this was the Prose Bowl! I felt pride swelling up, catching in my throat. Then clips of me began to appear on the TriDim screen, interspersed with ones of The Cranker, both of us in action, our words and sentences appearing high on the glistening boards, and the voices of Winkle and Sheldrake spoke of all my accomplishments, of how I was the youngest wordsmith ever to appear in the Prose Bowl, and I remembered what I'd thought in the Ultradome earlier in the week, about the place where a prosemaker created his prose being untouchable by anything or anyone, about a prosemaker being able to write true and fine, to *win*, no matter what might have happened to him. And suddenly the pride and the excitement overwhelmed all my other emotions, drowned and washed away the ambivalence, the questions about who and what I was, all the events of recent days.

The man named Rex Sackett was washed away too; in his place was the pulpeteer known as The Metaphor Kid.

I switched off the TriDim and sat down to wait for one of the Editors to come and tell me it was time to make my entrance. I didn't have to wait long; the knock sounded on the door after less than ten minutes. When the computer-lock released I caught up my Fuel container and stepped out, and together with the Editor I walked confidently down the tunnel toward the field.

I was ready for The Cranker now.

The Metaphor Kid was ready for the Big Face-Off.

2

A shower of roses and an ear-splitting mixture of cheers and applause greeted me when I emerged from the tunnel and trotted in along the sidelines. Sally and the folks and the rest of the Boosters were on their feet over in G Section, waving red and white pennants and yelling *"Sackett! Sackett! Sackett!"* at the top of their voices. The band struck up my old school song; I felt my eyes dampen as I stopped near my bench to listen and acknowledge the welcome with upraised Fuel container.

After the commotion and the music died down my Servos clustered around me, smoothing my uniform jersey, running hand-vacs over it, flexing my fingers in that way New-Sport Servos have to keep them nimble. Meanwhile, I looked across the field at the opposite sidelines and The Cranker's bench. But he hadn't made his appearance yet; his Servos were all standing in a military row, waiting.

A gaily dressed marching band, with half a dozen baton-twirling majorettes leading it, pranced out onto the northern end of the field—the last of the pre-game entertainment, one of my Servos told me. I took another couple of ounces of Fuel, felt it slide and glide through me and sharpen my thoughts, give them that bright clarity a pulpeteer needs if he's going to write a strong competitive match. Then I did a few short wind sprints to keep my leg muscles loose.

The scoreboard chronometers said there were less than

ten minutes to Face-Off when The Cranker finally came out of his tunnel at a slow plodding trot. The cheers that greeted him seemed even louder than the ones for me, and yet I thought I could hear a few catcalls mixed in too. Culp didn't seem to pay any attention either way. He just kept moving until he reached his bench, then stood motionless, almost statue-like, holding his Fuel container in both hands as his Servos swarmed around him.

I tamped tobacco into my old briar, waved my Servos off, and fired it myself with my laserflame lighter. I was feeling a lot of different things right then: excitement, pride, tension, and maybe just a touch of fear. Dealing with The Cranker in the Ultradome or at a TriDim press conference was one thing; dealing with him out here, in the Prose Bowl, was another thing altogether. The fact was, I couldn't seem to shake that lingering sense of awe I'd always had for him and his ability, his perseverance in hacking it out at or near the top as he had all these years. This wasn't any ordinary pro I was about to go up against. This was a legend known as The Cranker.

But I couldn't afford to let that rattle me; and I wouldn't, either. I squeezed my eyes shut, opened my mouth wide, took several deep breaths, and forced my mind to empty out all thoughts one by one—the old trick of mine to mentally pre-pare myself for a match. I would have liked another few ounces of Fuel, too, but I'd already reached my pre-game limit. Exceeding it was liable to do me more harm than good.

The Head Editor and the rest of the officials made their way out to the Line: It was almost time for the Face-Off to begin. The P.A. announcer introduced me first, because I was wearing the visitor's red, and I stepped out and waved at the packed stands. There was a chorus of cheers, particularly from over in G Section, that lasted a full half minute. The ovation for The Cranker, when his name was announced, lasted at least that long—but again, I thought I could hear a faint un-dercurrent of booing, as if there was a vocal minority of fans who resented Culp or still felt he was a washed-up old hack in spite of what he'd done to Fast-Action Eddie Duke last week.

The Cranker, though, just stood as motionless as he had on the sidelines, his seamed face set in stoic determination. Maybe some of the fans felt he was washed up, but in his blue uniform jersey, outlined against the hot New Year's sky, he looked bigger to me than he really was—awesome, implacable. Unbeatable.

Everybody stood up as the marching band played the National Anthem. Then there was another uproar from the fans—I'd never imagined just how deafening it could get down here on the floor of the Prose Bowl—and finally the Head Editor called us over for the coin flip. I called tails in the air, and the coin fell to the turf and came up tails. The Head Editor moved over to me and patted my shoulders to indicate I'd won the toss; the Sackett Boosters bellowed their approval. Through all of this, Culp remained unmoving and aloof, not looking at me or the Head Editor or anything else, it seemed.

We went to the Line and got ready. I was becoming more and more tense as the Face-Off neared; the palms of my hands were slick and my head seemed suddenly empty. What if I can't think of a title? I thought. What if I can't think of an opening sentence?

"Be cool, kid," Mort had told me once. "Don't try to force it. The words'll come, just like they always have." I didn't want to think about Mort ever again, but the advice was sound; I made myself concentrate on that, not on who'd given it to me.

The Cranker and I stood facing each other, looking at the scoreboards at opposite ends of the field. Then, out of the corner of my eye, I saw the Head Editor wave his red starting flag at the Line Editor; and in the next instant the two plot topics selected by the officials flashed on the boards.

A. FUTURISTIC LOVE-ADVENTURE
B. MID-TWENTIETH-CENTURY DETECTIVE

I had five seconds to make my choice. Both of the topics looked tough, but this was the Prose Bowl and nothing came easy in the championship. I'd always been a little stronger at Suspense Fic than Futuristic Fic, so I yelled out "Plot B!" to the Head Editor. He unfurled his white flag with the letter B on it, and immediately the P.A. announcer's voice boomed, "The Metaphor Kid chooses Plot B!"

The crowd broke into thunderous applause; the sound of it was like a pressure against my eardrums. I could feel my pulse racing in hard irregular rhythm and my stomach was knotted up. I tried not to think about the fifty million people watching me on the TriDim close-ups.

The Line Editor's claxon went off.

The Cranker and I broke for our machines. And all of a sudden, as I was sliding into my chair, I felt control and a kind of calm come into me. That was the way it always was with me, the way it always was with the great ones, everybody said: No matter how nervous you were before the start of a match, once the horn sounded your professionalism took over and you forgot everything except the job you had to do.

I had a title even before I reached for the first sheet of paper beside the typewriter: THE MICAWBER DIAMOND. And I had the first sentence, the narrative hook, as soon as I rolled the sheet into the platen.

SAM SLEDGE WAS POURING HIS MORNING EYE-OPENER WITH ONE HAND, OILING HIS .45 WITH THE OTHER, WHEN THE COPS CAME AND TOLD HIM HIS PARTNER MILES CHANDLER HAD BEEN MURDERED.

The place deep inside where the prose comes from was wide open now: I was already starting to think two sentences ahead of what was rushing out through my fingers. My second paragraph was almost complete before I heard Culp's machine begin its amplified hammering across the Line.

A hundred thousand voices screamed for speed and continuity. I hunched forward, teeth locked around the stem of my briar, and drove through two more paragraphs of stage-setting. End of page one. I glanced up at the south-end scoreboard as I ripped the sheet out of the platen and rolled in a new one.

SACKETT 226, CULP 187.

I laid in half a page of flashback, working the adjectives and the adverbs to build up my count, powered through eight lines of descriptive transition, and came into the first passage of dialogue. Up on the board, what I was writing appeared in foot-high printout, as if the words were emblazoned on the sky itself.

SLEDGE STALKED ACROSS HIS PLUSH OFFICE, LEAVING FOOTPRINTS IN THE THICK SHAG CARPET LIKE ANGRY DOUGHNUTS. VELDA VANCE, ALLUR-INGLY BEAUTIFUL SECRETARY TO SLEDGE AND CHANDLER INVESTIGATIONS, LOOKED UP IN ALARM. "SOMEBODY MURDERED MILES CHANDLER LAST NIGHT," SLEDGE GRITTED TO HER, "AND STOLE THE MICAWBER DIAMOND HE WAS GUARD-ING."

It was solid stuff, I knew that. Not my best but plenty good enough and just what the fans wanted. The sound of my name echoing through the great stadium put chills on my back.

"Sackett! Hack it! Sackett, hack it! Sackett hack it Sackett hack it Sackett hack it!"

I finished the last line on page two and had the clean sheet into the machine in two seconds flat. My eyes found the scoreboard again as I pounded the keys: SACKETT 529, CULP 430. Hundred-word lead, but that was nothing in this early going. Without losing speed or concentration, I sneaked a look at what The Cranker was punching out.

THE DENEBIAN GREEN-BEAST CAME TOWARD HER, MOVING WITH A CURIOUSLY FLOWING MO-TION, ITS TENTACLES SWAYING IN A SENSUAL DANCE OF ALIEN LUST. SHE STOOD FROZEN AGAINST A RUDDER OF ROCK AND STARED AT THE THING IN HORROR. THE UNDULATING TENTACLES REACHED TOWARD HER AND THE GREEN WAVES OF DAMP WHICH THE BEAST EXUDED SENT SHUDDERS THROUGH HER RIGID FLESH.

God, I thought, that's top-line prose. He's as inspired as he was last week against Fast-Action Eddie; he's pulling out all the stops.

The crowd sensed it too. I could hear his cheerleaders chanting, almost drowning out the cries from my own rooters across the way.

"Come on, Culp! Write that pulp!"

I was in the most intense struggle of my life, there was no doubt about that. I'd known it was going to be rough, but knowing it and then being in the middle of it were two different things. The Cranker was a legend in his own time; when he was right, as he had been last week, no one had his facility, his speed, his edge with the cutting transitions, his ability to produce under stress. If he could maintain pace and narrative drive, there wasn't a pulpeteer on earth who could beat him—

SACKETT 920, CULP 874.

The score registered on my mind and I realized with a jolt that my own pace had slacked off: Culp had cut my lead by more than half. That was what happened to you when you started worrying about your opponent and what he was doing: you ended up mind-psyching yourself. I could hear Mort's voice again, echoing in my memory, saying, "The pressure will turn your head if you let it. But I don't think it ever will. I think you're made of the real stuff, kid; I think you've got the guts and the heart."

THE ANGER ON MICAWBER'S FACE MELTED AWAY LIKE SOAP IN A SOAP DISH UNDER A STREAM OF HOT DIRTY WATER.

I jammed out that line and I knew I was back in the groove, beginning to crank near the top of my form. The sound of my machine climbed to a staccato pulse. Dialogue, some fast foreshadowing, a string of four adjectives that drew a burst of applause from the Boosters. I could feel my wrists starting to knot up from the strain, and there was pain in my left leg where I'd pulled the hamstring. But I didn't pay any attention to that; I had written in pain before and I wasn't about to let it bother me now. I just kept firing out my prose.

Only I wasn't gaining back any of my lead, I saw then. The foot-high numerals read SACKETT 1163, CULP 1127. The Cranker had hit his stride and he was matching me word for word, sentence for sentence.

SHE HAD NO MORE STRENGTH LEFT TO RUN. SHE WAS TRAPPED NOW, THERE WAS NO ESCAPE. A SCREAM BURST FROM HER THROAT AS THE BEAST BOUNDED UP TO HER AND DREW HER INTO ITS AWFUL CLUTCHES, BREATHING GREEN FUMES AGAINST THE FACEPLATE OF HER SUIT. IT WAS GOING TO WORK ITS WILL ON HER! IT WAS GOING TO DO UNSPEAKABLE THINGS TO HER BODY!

"Culp, Culp, Culp!"

THE NIGHT WAS DARK AND WET AND COLD AND THE RAIN FELL ON SLEDGE LIKE A MILLION TEARS FROM A MILLION LOST LOVES ON A MILLION WORLDS IN A MILLION GALAXIES.

"Sackett, Sackett, Sackett!"

Sweat streamed into my eyes, made the numerals on the board seem smeared and glistening: SACKETT 1895, CULP 1857. I ducked my head against the sleeve of my jersey and slid a new sheet into the machine. On the other side of the Line, The Cranker was sitting straight and stiff behind his typewriter, fingers flying, his shaggy head wreathed in cigarette smoke. But he wasn't just hitting the keys, he was *attacking* them—as if they, not me, were the enemy and he was trying to club them into submission.

I reached back for a little extra, raced through the rest of the transition, slammed out three paragraphs of introspection and five more of dialogue. New page. More dialogue, then another narrative hook to foreshadow the first confrontation scene. New page. Description and some cat-and-mouse action to build suspense.

AS HE WAITED IN THE DARK ALLEY FOR THE GUY WHO WAS FOLLOWING HIM, SLEDGE'S RIGHT HAND ITCHED AROUND THE .45 IN HIS POCKET. HE COULD FEEL THE OLD FAMILIAR RAGE BURNING IN-

SIDE HIM, MAKING HIS BLOOD BOIL LIKE WATER IN
A KETTLE ON THE OLD WOOD-BURNING STOVE IN
HIS OLD MAN'S FOURTH-FLOOR WALK-UP IN THE
OLD

My machine locked. I heard the cheering rise to a cre-
scendo; two hundred thousand hands commenced clapping as
the Line Editor's horn blared.

End of the first quarter.

SACKETT 2500, CULP 2473.

3

I leaned back in my chair, sleeving more wetness from my face, and did some deep breathing. The Cranker got to his feet. He stood in a rigid posture, a fresh cigarette burning between his lips, and squinted toward the sidelines. His Servos were already on the field, running toward him with water bucket and a container of Fuel.

My own Servos reached me a short time later. One of them extended Fuel, but even though my mouth was dry, sandy, I shook my head and gestured him away. I'd decided I would hold off on the Fuel during the match itself for as long as possible; it was part of the game plan I'd worked out at the hotel.

By the time I finished splashing water on my face and toweling off, there was less than a minute of the time-out left. I looked over at G Section. I couldn't pick Sally out of the bright sea of faces, or Mom or Dad either, but just knowing they were there was enough.

I took my place at the Line, knocked dottle out of the briar, tamped in some fresh tobacco, and fired it. My mind was racing again, working ahead—a full four sentences when Culp stood ready and the Head Editor raised the red starting flag.

Claxon.

I lunged for my machine, started typing almost before I settled into the chair.

NEIGHBORHOOD. THE FOLLOWER HAD SOME-
THING TO DO WITH HIS PARTNER'S MURDER AND
THE THEFT OF THE MICAWBER DIAMOND, SLEDGE
WAS SURE OF THAT. HE WAS GOING TO GET SOME
ANSWERS NOW, EVEN IF HE HAD TO START SHOOT-
ING PEOPLE TO DO IT.

And I was off, banging away at the same feverish pace of
the first period. I cut through a full page of action, interspers-
ing it with dialogue, drawing it out; the scene was good for
another five hundred words, at least. My pipe went out at the
end of page eleven and without thinking about it I did my
trick of relighting it with one hand while I slid fresh paper
into the platen and typed a fast sentence with the other hand.
The fans loved it; it got me another standing ovation from the
Sackett Boosters.

Twelve pages down then and the thirteenth in the typewriter. My quality level was still good, but when I glanced up
at the board I saw that The Cranker was once again cranking
at the top of his game.

BUT EVEN WHILE SHE WAS CLINGING TO THE
STARFLEET CAPTAIN WHO HAD SAVED HER LIFE,
SHE FELT A STRANGE SADNESS. THE GREEN-BEAST
HAD BEEN DISINTEGRATED AND WAS NOTHING
MORE NOW THAN A PUDDLE OF GREEN ON THE
DUSTY SANDS OF DENEB, LIKE A SPLOTCH OF PAINT
ON AN ALIEN CANVAS. THE HORROR WAS OVER. AND
YET . . . AND YET, DESPITE HER REVULSION, THE
THING HAD STIRRED SOMETHING DEEP AND PRIMI-
TIVE INSIDE HER THAT SHE WAS ONLY JUST BEGIN-
NING TO UNDERSTAND.

"Culp, Culp—grind that pulp!"

My lead had dwindled to a mere twelve words: the scoreboard read SACKETT 3359, CULP 3347. The Cranker was
making his move now, and he was doing it despite the fact
that I was working at maximum speed.

The feeling of tension and uncertainty began to gnaw at
me again. I fought it down, concentrated even more intensely,

punching the keys so hard that pain shot up both wrists. Fresh sweat rolled off me; the hot California sun lay on the back of my neck like a burning hand.

SLEDGE SNARLED, "YOU'LL TALK, ALL RIGHT!" AND SWATTED THE GUY ACROSS THE SIDE OF THE HEAD WITH HIS .45. THE GUY REELED AND STAG-GERED INTO THE WET ALLEY WALL. SLEDGE MOVED IN, TRANSFERRING THE ROD TO HIS LEFT HAND. HE HIT THE FOLLOWER A SECOND TIME, HIT HIM IN THE MOUTH WITH A HAND LIKE A FIST

The Head Editor's whistle blew.

And my typewriter locked, jamming my fingers.

Penalty. Penalty!

My throat closed up. I snapped my head over toward the officials' table on the sidelines and saw the ten-second penalty flag waving—the green-and-black one that meant Phrasing Unacceptable. The crowd was making a magnified sound that was half-excited, half-groaning; I knew the TriDim cameras would have homed in on me for a series of close-ups, that Vinnie Winkle and Lloyd Sheldrake would be making all sorts of speculations over the instant replays. I could feel my face reddening. First penalty of the match and I had let it happen to me.

But that wasn't the worst part. The worst part was that it was going to cost me the lead: The Cranker's machine was still clattering on at white heat, churning out words and sen-tences that flashed like taunts on the board.

I counted off the seconds in my mind, and when the Head Editor's flag dropped and my machine unlocked, I flailed the keys angrily, rewriting the penalty sentence: HE HIT THE FOLLOWER A SECOND TIME, HIT HIM IN THE MOUTH WITH A HAND LIKE A CEMENT BLOCK. But the damage had been done, all right. The board told me that and told everyone else too.

CULP 3899, SACKETT 3878.

The penalty seemed to have energized The Cranker, given him a psychological lift; he was working faster than ever now, with even more savagery. I felt a little wrench of fear. About the only way you could beat one of the greats was to take the lead early and hold it. Once an experienced old prosemaker like Culp got in front, the advantage was all his.

A quote dropped into my mind, one I'd read a long time ago in an Old-Sport history text, and it made me shiver: "Going up against the best is a little bit like going up against Death."

I had my own speed back now, but my concentration wasn't as sharp as it had been before the penalty; a couple of times I hit the wrong keys, misspelled words and then had to retype them. It was just the kind of penalty reaction Mort had warned me against early on in my career. "Penalties don't mean a thing," he'd said. "What you've got to watch out for is worrying about them, letting them dam up the flow or lead you into another mistake."

But Mort had betrayed me, Mort was in jail: It wasn't Mort out here in the hot Prose Bowl sun, going head-to-head against a legend. . . .

The amplified sound of Culp's machine seemed louder than my own, steadier, more rhythmic. Nervously I checked the board again. His stuff was coming so fast now that it might have been written by one of the experimental prose-computers instead of a pulpeteer.

SHE LOOKED OUT THROUGH THE SHIP'S VIEW-SCREEN AT THE EMPTY SWEEP OF SPACE. BEHIND HER SHE COULD HEAR THE CAPTAIN TALKING TO THE BASE COMMANDER AT EARTH COLONY SEVEN, RELAYING THE INFORMATION ABOUT THE SHUT-TLE-SHIP CRASH ON DENEB. "ONLY ONE SURVIVOR," HE WAS SAYING. YES, SHE THOUGHT, ONLY ONE SUR-VIVOR. BUT I WISH THERE HADN'T BEEN ANY SUR-VIVORS. IF I'D DIED IN THE CRASH TOO, THEN I WOULDN'T HAVE BEEN ATTACKED BY THE GREEN-BEAST. AND I WOULDN'T BE FEELING THESE STRANGE AND TERRIBLE EMOTIONS, THIS SENSE OF UNFULFILLMENT AND DEPRIVATION.

Some of the fans were on their feet, screaming *"Cranker! Cranker!"*

CULP 4250, SACKETT 4196.

And over in G Section, the Boosters waved their pennants and chanted *"Now's the time, Kid! So make your bid!"*

I felt light-headed, giddy with tension; but the adrenalin kept flowing and the words kept coming, pouring out of my subconscious and through the mind haze and out into the blazing afternoon—nouns, verbs, adjectives, adverbs. Don't let him gain any more ground. Stay close. Stay close!

SLEDGE FOLLOWED THE FAT MAN THROUGH THE HEAVY DARKNESS ALONG THE RIVER. THE STENCH OF FISH AND MUD AND GARBAGE WAFTED UP FROM THE OILY BLACK WATER AND SLAPPED HIM ACROSS THE FACE LIKE A DIRTY WET TOWEL. HE DIDN'T KNOW WHERE THE FAT MAN WAS LEADING HIM, BUT I FELT SURE IT

Whistle.

Lock.

Penalty.

I looked up in disbelief and saw the Head Editor waving the purple-and-gold penalty flag that signified Switched Person. A smattering of boos rolled down around me from the stands. My eyes flicked to the board, and it was true, I had slipped out of third person and into first—an amateur's mistake, a kid's blunder. Shame made me duck my head; it was as if, in that moment, I could feel concentrated waves of disgust from the hundred million eyes that watched me.

The ten seconds of the penalty were like a hundred, a thousand. Because all the while The Cranker's machine ratcheted onward, not once slowing or breaking cadence. When my typewriter finally unlocked I redid the sentence in the proper person and plunged ahead without checking the score. I didn't want to know how far behind I was now. I was afraid that if I did know, it would make me reckless with urgency and push me into another stupid error.

My throat was parched, raw, and hot from the pipe

smoke, and for the first time since the match began I thought about the Fuel. It had been a long time since I'd wanted it with such sudden yearning in the first half of a face-off. Only I couldn't have it, not until halftime, not without taking a disastrous twenty-second Fuel penalty. There had to be less than six hundred words left to the end of the quarter, I told myself; I could hold out that long. A top-line pro could do six hundred words no matter what the circumstances. A top-line pro, as The Cranker himself had once said, could do six hundred words *dead.*

I forced myself to shut out everything from my mind except the prose, the story line. Old page out of the platen, new page in. Old page out, new page in. Speed, speed, but make sure of the grammar, the tense, the person, the phrasing. Still a full five thousand words to go in the match. Still an even chance for a second-half comeback.

THE INTERIOR OF THE WAREHOUSE WAS DANK AND MUSTY AND FILLED WITH CROUCHING SHADOWS LIKE A PLATOON OF EVIL SPIRITS WAITING TO LEAP ON HIM. THEN THERE WAS A FLICKER OF LIGHT AT THE REAR AND IT TOLD SLEDGE THE FAT MAN HAD SWITCHED ON A SMALL POCKET FLASH. ROSCOE IN HAND, FINGER TIGHT ON THE TRIGGER, HE CREPT STEALTHILY TOWARD THE

My machine locked again.

I jerked my head up, half expecting to see a penalty flag aloft for the third time. But it wasn't a penalty; it was halftime at last. The Line Editor's horn blew. The Cranker's cheering section was chanting *"Culp! Culp! Culp!"*

I had to look at the board then, at the score shining against the sky, and I did.

CULP 5000, SACKETT 4796.

4

Some of the tension drained out of me and I sat there feeling limp, heavy with fatigue. The joints in my fingers were stiff; there was a spot of blood on the tip of my right forefinger where the skin had split near the nail. But the score was all that mattered to me at that moment, and it wasn't as bad as I'd feared. I had made up larger margins than that in my career; I could do it again.

I could still win.

Across the Line, Culp was on his feet and staring down at the turf with eyes that gleamed and didn't blink. He wasn't quite so imposing now, strangely. His back was bowed and his hands looked a little shaky—as though he was the one who was trailing by 204 words and facing an uphill battle in the second half.

When I pushed back my own chair and stood up, a sudden sharp pain in my tender hamstring made me clutch at the table edge. I was soaked in sweat and so thirsty I had trouble swallowing. But I didn't reach for the Fuel when my Servos appeared; in spite of my need I didn't want to take any while I was out here on the field, didn't want to show The Cranker and the fans and the TriDim audience that I needed it as badly as I did. In the locker room, yes. It was only a few more minutes.

Two of Culp's Servos began escorting him off the field toward the tunnel at the south end, where the home locker room was located; he was hanging onto his Fuel container with both hands again. I waved away my people and hobbled toward the north tunnel alone.

More roses showered me as I came into the tunnel. That was a good sign; the fans hadn't given up on me. The passageway was cool, a welcome relief from the blazing sun, and empty except for the League official and the security Servos who were stationed there to keep out fans, scribes, and anyone else who might try to see me. The Prose Bowl rules were strict: Each of the contestants had to spend halftime alone, locked in his respective locker room without typewriter or any other kind of writing tools. Back in '15, the year of the Postal-Rate Riots, a pro named Penny-A-Word Gordon had been disqualified for cheating when officials found out another wordsmith, hired by Gordon's agent, had written a fast one-thousand-word continuation during the break and delivered it to Gordon, who then revised it with a pen, memorized it, and used it to build up an early third-quarter lead. The incident had caused a pretty large scandal at the time, and the Prose Bowl people weren't about to let it or something like it happen again.

As soon as I entered the locker room, the door panel whispered shut and locked itself electronically. But I was already on my way to where a fresh container of Fuel sat waiting on the desk. I measured out three ounces, tossed it off, and waited for it to work its magic. It didn't take long; the last of the tension and most of the lassitude were gone within seconds. I poured out another three ounces, set it aside, and stripped off my sodden uniform.

While the Body-Ease massaged my sore leg and thermoshowered me, I thought about The Cranker. His performance in the first half had been flawless: no penalties, unflagging speed, front-line prose. It hadn't been as dazzling as the one against Fast-Action Eddie, but then he was working Futuristic Fic now, not Quality Lit, and he couldn't use stream-of-consciousness or pyrotechnical technique to quite the same degree. Even his detractors wouldn't be able to find fault with the way he was going, or even the slightest indication that he was about to wilt under the pressure.

So if I was going to beat him I had to do it on talent and speed and desire—all on my own. Nothing came easy in this business or in the Prose Bowl; I'd known that all along. You had to work long and hard if you wanted to win. You had to give your all, and try to stay away from the penalties, and fight off all the outside pressures, and hope that you were good enough and strong enough to come out on top.

No, The Cranker wasn't going to beat himself. And I wasn't going to beat myself either.

When the Body-Ease finished drying and deodorizing me I stepped out and put on a clean uniform. Then I bandaged the wound on my forefinger and took the rest of my allotted Fuel an ounce at a time, savoring it. I could feel my confidence building, solidifying again.

The chronometer on one wall said that there were still nine minutes left in the time-out. I paced around, flexing my leg to keep the hamstring from retightening. It was quiet in there, almost too quiet; I thought about putting on the Tri-Dim and watching the halftime highlights and listening to what Winkle and Sheldrake were saying about me. But I decided I didn't want to know what they were saying. I wasn't even sure I cared.

The silence seemed to press down on me, made me think again, as I had often lately of how alone I was. I wished Mort was there—the Mort of old, the Mort I'd trusted—so we could discuss strategy for the second half; I wished the folks and Sally were there so I could tell them how I felt, how self-assured I was.

But would it really make a difference? I thought then. Would they really understand? The answer to both questions was no; I had to admit it. You were always alone in the pros, that was the inescapable thing. Your parents, the girl you loved, your agent, the fans—all of them gave you as much help and support as they could; but they weren't pulpeteers and they just didn't know what it was like to go out time after time and face the machine, the blank sheets of paper, the pressure and pain of millions of words and hundreds of face-offs. The only ones who did know what it was like were other pros; only your own could truly understand.

Only your own.

The Cranker?

Were we really opponents, enemies? Or were we soul brothers, bound more closely than any blood relatives because we shared the same basic loneliness?

Were he and I—all pulpeteers—the same?

Was New-Sport corrupt and meaningless?

These were unnerving thoughts and I pushed them out of my head before they could become entrenched in there and cut into my concentration for the second half. I couldn't go out there and face Culp believing we were one and the same, believing the Prose Bowl was without honor or significance. It would be like going up against myself, in one sense, trying to overcome myself in a contest that no one could ever win. . . .

The door panel unlocked finally, just as the three-minute warning horn blew, and I hurried out of the locker room. One of the Editors was waiting for me; I followed him down the tunnel past the silent security Servos and back into the stadium. The last of the marching bands and majorettes were just filing off onto the sidelines, ending the halftime festivities. The fans were buzzing, and when they saw me emerge and lope out toward the Line, there was another cascade of roses and a fresh burst of cheering, and the Sackett band began once more to play my old school song.

Culp wasn't there yet. But as I reached the cluster of Servos around my bench, I heard the roar from the stands intensify and his rooting section set up a chant: *"Cranker! Cranker!"* There were no catcalls this time, or at least none that I could hear. Then I saw him, coming out of the south tunnel, not running but walking in a loose rapid gait. Halfway out, he seemed to stagger just a little, then regained his stride. When he stopped near his own bench, one of his Servos tried to take his Fuel container; Culp shoved him away and clutched it possessively. I wondered how much Fuel he'd had during the time-out. Not that it mattered; it wouldn't have been enough to make a difference.

The Head Editor walked out carrying his flags. I walked out too and took my place at the Line. The Cranker finally relinquished his Fuel container, ran a gnarled hand over his mouth, and moved out to face me. His eyes, I saw then, were bright and fixed, like shiny nailheads in a block of old gray wood.

I lit my pipe and Culp fired a cigarette; we were both ready. The crowd noise subsided as the Head Editor raised his red flag—and then surged again as the flag fell and the claxon sounded.

The second half was underway.

5

My mind was clear and sharp as I dropped into my chair. I had checked my prose printout, waiting at the Line, and I had the rest of my unfinished sentence and the rest of the paragraph already worked out; I punched it down, followed it with three fast paragraphs of descriptive narrative. Build into another action-confrontation scene? No. I was only at the halfway point in the story line and it would throw my pacing off. I laid in a deft one-line twist, for shock value, and cut away into transition.

"That's it, Sackett! That's how to hack it!"

The approving cheers from the Boosters and from the rest of the fans were like a fresh shot of Fuel: I could feel my thoughts expanding, settling squarely into the groove. Words poured out of me; phrases, sentences, crisp images, the kind of multi-line metaphors that had given me my nickname. The beat of my typewriter was steady, unrelieved, like a peal of thunder rolling across the clear blue sky.

But it wasn't the only thunder in the Prose Bowl, I realized abruptly. The Cranker's machine was making it too—louder, faster, even more intense. For the first time since the quarter began I glanced up at the board.

CULP 6132, SACKETT 5898.

I couldn't believe it. I had been certain that I was cutting into his lead, that I had closed to within at least a hundred and seventy-five words; instead Culp had widened the margin by another thirty.

"OH YES, CAPTAIN!" SHE MURMURED. "OH YES, YES, OH CAPTAIN, OH YES, OH PLEASE CAPTAIN, OH, OH!" BUT EVEN AS SHE SPOKE THE WORDS, EVEN AS SHE WRITHED IN THE CAPTAIN'S STRONG MAS-CULINE EMBRACE, IT WAS NOT FINGERS SHE IMAG-INED CARESSING HER FEVERED FLESH, IT WAS TENTACLES. . . .

The thin edge of fear cut at me again, slicing through the confidence and that feeling of controlled power I always had when I was going good. I was throwing everything I had at The Cranker here in the third period, and it wasn't good enough—he was still writing masterful prose, he was still pull-ing away.

I bit down so hard on the stem of my briar that I felt it crack between my teeth. Keep bearing down, I told myself grimly. Don't let up for a second. You can still catch him; you're not out of this yet.

HE WAS STILL THINKING ABOUT THE CASE, TRY-ING TO PUT THE PIECES OF THE PUZZLE TOGETHER, WHEN THE TELEPHONE RANG. IT WAS VELDA. "I'VE BEEN WORRIED ABOUT YOU, SAM," HER SOFT PURR-ING VOICE SAID, AND ALL OF A SUDDEN HE FELT A BURNING, OVERWHELMING NEED TO SEE HER. SHE WAS THE ONLY PERSON HE COULD TALK TO, THE ONE PERSON IN THE WORLD WHO UNDERSTOOD WHAT IT WAS LIKE TO BE A PRIVATE DICK.

"Sackett, Sackett!"

But The Cranker's machine kept on soaring; The Cranker's words kept on racing across the board with relent-less speed.

WHEN SHE WAS SURE THE CAPTAIN WAS ASLEEP SHE GOT OUT OF THE BUNK AND PADDED OVER TO WHERE HIS UNIFORM LAY. SHE KNEW WHAT SHE HAD TO DO NOW. SHE ACCEPTED THE TRUTH AT LAST, BECAUSE THE WHOLE TIME SHE

HAD BEEN COPULATING WITH THE CAPTAIN HER
THOUGHTS HAD BEEN BACK ON DENEB, FULL OF
THE SIGHT AND THE SMELL OF GREEN.

"Culp, Culp, Culp!"

The lift from the six ounces of Fuel I'd had in the locker
room was gone now and the tension was back, binding the
muscles in my fingers and shoulders. The sun seemed to be
getting hotter, drawing runnels of sweat from my pores, making my head throb. My words were still coming fast, but the
images weren't quite as sharp as they'd been minutes ago, the
metaphors not quite as clean, the quality level not quite as
high. I didn't care. Speed was all that mattered now; I was
willing to sacrifice quality for the maintenance of speed.

CULP 6912, SACKETT 6671.

Down by 241 now; The Cranker had only gained seven
words in the last eight hundred. But *he* had gained them, not
me—I couldn't seem to narrow his lead, no matter what I did.
I lifted my head, still typing furiously, and stared across at
him. His teeth were bared; sweat glistened like oil on his gray
skin. Yet his fingers were a sunlit blur on the keys, as if they
were independent creatures performing a mad sort of dance.

CLENCHING THE CAPTAIN'S LASER WEAPON IN
HER HAND, SHE MADE HER WAY AFT TO WHERE
THE LIFECRAFT WERE KEPT. SHE KNEW THE COOR-
DINATES FOR DENEB. SHE WOULD ORDER THE LIFE-
CRAFT'S COMPUTER TO TAKE HER THERE—TAKE
HER TO THE PROMISE OF THE GREEN.

A feeling of desperation came into me. Time was running
out; there were less than five hundred words left to go in the
quarter, less than three thousand left in the match. You could
make up two hundred and fifty words in the fourth period of a
face-off, but you couldn't do it unless you had momentum.
And I didn't have it, I couldn't seem to get it. It all belonged
to The Cranker.

The fans continued to shriek, creating a wild counter-
point to the thunder of our machines. I imagined I could hear

Dad's voice telling me to hold on, keep cranking, and Mom's voice hoarse from shouting, and Sally's voice saying "You can do it, darling, you can do it!"

CULP 7245, SACKETT 7002.

Holding. Down two hundred and forty-five now, but holding.

You can do it, you can do it!

SLEDGE'S EYES GLOWED AS HE LOOKED AT VELDA'S MAGNIFICENT BOSOM. VELDA, THE ONLY WOMAN HE'D WANTED SINCE HIS WIFE LEFT HIM THREE YEARS AGO BECAUSE SHE COULDN'T STAND HIM BEING A SHAMUS AND HAVING TO DEAL WITH THE DREGS OF HUMANITY ALL THE TIME. THE PALMS OF HIS HANDS WERE WET, HOT AND WET WITH DESIRE.

The palms of my hands were hot and wet, but I didn't dare take the time to wipe them dry. Only a hundred and fifty to go in the quarter now.

HE TOOK HER INTO HIS ARMS. THE FEEL OF HER VOLUPTUOUS BODY WAS EXQUISITE. HE CRUSHED HIS MOUTH AGAINST HERS, HEARD HER MOAN AS HIS HAND CAME UP AND SLID ACROSS THE SUC- CULENT CURVE OF HER BREAST.

"TAKE ME, SAM," SHE BREATHED HUSKILY AGAINST HIS LIPS. "TEAR MY CLOTHES OFF AND GIVE ME YOUR HOT

I tore page twenty-six out of the typewriter, slapped in page twenty-seven.

LOVE. GIVE IT TO ME NOW, SAM!"

SLEDGE WANTED TO DO JUST THAT. BUT SOME- THING HELD HIM BACK. THEN HE HEARD IT—A SOUND OUT IN THE HALLWAY, A FURTIVE SCRAB- BLING SOUND LIKE A RAT MAKES. YEAH, HE THOUGHT, A HUMAN RAT. HE LET GO OF VELDA, PULLED OUT HIS .45, AND SPUN AROUND IN A CROUCH.

My machine locked the instant after I touched the period key; the Line Editor's horn sounded.

The third quarter was over.

I sagged in my chair, only half aware of the crowd noise swelling around me, and peered up at the board. The printout and the numerals blazed like lines and curves of fire in the sunlight.

CULP 7500, SACKETT 7255.

6

A deepening fatigue seeped through me, dulling my thoughts. Dimly I saw The Cranker leaning forward across his machine, head cradled in his arms; his whole body heaved as if he couldn't get enough air into his lungs. What were Vinnie Winkle and Lloyd Sheldrake saying about him on the TriDim telecast? Did they believe he could maintain his grueling pace for another full quarter? Did they think I still had a chance to win?

Did anyone think I still had a chance to win?

Down 245 now with only twenty-five hundred left. . . .

Culp took his Fuel sitting down this time, with his head tilted back and his throat working spasmodically. I did the same; I felt that if I stood up my knees would buckle and I would sprawl out like a clown. The game plan called for no more than three ounces at the third-quarter break—none at all if I could hold off—but I hadn't counted on being down as far as I was at this point in the match. I took a full six ounces, praying it would shore up my flagging strength, and even then I had to force myself not to make it nine or ten.

Only it didn't do anything for me, as it had at halftime and as it usually did in competition. No lift at all. My mind remained sluggish and the muscles in my arms and wrists wouldn't relax. The only effect it had was to make my head pound and my stomach feel kind of queasy.

With a minute of the time-out left I loaded my pipe

again, put the laserflame to it. The smoke tasted foul and made my head throb all the more painfully. I laid the pipe down and did some slow deep breathing. On his side of the Line Culp was lighting a fresh cigarette off the butt of an old one. He looked shrunken now, at least ten years older than his age of fifty-seven—not formidable at all.

You don't awe me anymore, I told him mentally, trying to psych myself up. I can beat you because I'm as good as you are, I'm *better* than you are. Better, old man, you hear me?

He didn't look at me. He hadn't looked at me once during the entire Face-Off.

The Head Editor's red flag went up. I poised on the balls of my feet, shaking my head in an effort to clear away some of the fuzziness. The screaming voices of the fans seemed almost hysterical, full of anticipation and a kind of hunger, like animals waiting for the kill.

All right, I thought, this is it.

The red flag dropped and the claxon blared and I broke for my machine, slid into my chair with my fingers coming down hard on the keyboard.

ALL RIGHT, SLEDGE THOUGHT, THIS IS IT. HE

And my mind went blank.

My hands started to tremble; body fluid streamed down my cheeks. Think of a sentence, for God's sake! But it was as if my brain had contracted, squeezed up into a tiny clotted mass that blocked off all subconscious connection.

The Cranker's machine was making thunder again.

HE

Nothing.

"Come on, Sackett! Hack it, hack it!"

HE

HE

Block. I was blocked.

Panic surged through me. I hadn't had a block since my first year in the Junior Creative League; I'd never believed it could happen to me in the Bigs. All the symptoms came rushing in on the heels of the panic: feeling of suffocation, pain in my chest, irregular breathing, nausea, strange sounds coming unbidden from my throat that were the beginnings, not the endings of words.

A volley of boos thudded against my eardrums, like rocks of sound stinging, hurting. I could feel myself starting to whimper; I had the terrible sensation of imminent collapse across my typewriter.

The stuttering roar of Culp's machine ceased for two or three seconds as he pulled out a completed page and inserted new paper, then began again with a vengeance.

A fragment of memory disgorged itself from the clotted mass inside my head: Mort's voice saying to me a long time ago, when he'd first taken me on as a client, "To break a block you begin at the beginning. Subject. Object. Noun. Verb. Preposition. Participle. Take one word at a time, build a sentence, and pretty soon the rest will come."

Subject.

Noun. Pronoun.

HE

Verb. Verb.

WENT

HE WENT

Preposition.

TO

HE WENT TO

Object.

THE DOOR

Period? No, not yet. Article.

AND

HE WENT TO THE DOOR AND

Action verb.

THREW IT OPEN AND THE FAT MAN WAS THERE, CROUCHED AT THE EDGE OF THE STAIRCASE, A GUN HELD IN HIS FAT FIST. SLEDGE FELT THE RAGE EXPLODE INSIDE HIM. HE DODGED OUT INTO THE HALLWAY, RAISING HIS .45. THE BIG MAN WOULD FEEL SLEDGE'S FIRE IN HIS FAT PRETTY SOON NOW.

"Sackett, Sackett, Sackett!"

It had all come back in a single wrenching flood; the feeling of mind-shrinkage was gone, and along with it the suffocation, the chest pain, the nausea. But the panic was still there. I had broken the momentary block, I was firing again at full speed, but how much time had I lost? How many more words had I fallen behind?

I was afraid to look up at the board. And yet I *had* to know the score, I had to know if I still had any kind of chance. Fearfully I lifted my eyes, blinking away sweat.

CULP 8015, SACKETT 7369.

The panic dulled and gave way to despair. Six hundred and forty-six words down, with less than two thousand to go and The Cranker showing no signs of weakening. Hopeless—it was hopeless.

I was going to lose.

Most of the fans were standing, urging Culp on with great booming cries of his name. They sounded even hungrier now, and it struck me then that they wanted to see him humiliate me, pour it on and scuff me by a thousand words or more. Well, I wasn't going to give them that satisfaction. I wouldn't be disgraced in front of my girl and family and fifty million TriDim viewers. I wouldn't quit, I wouldn't go down without fighting to the last possible second.

In a frenzy I pounded out the last few lines on page thirty, ripped it free and replaced it. Action, action—draw the scene out for at least three more pages. Adjectives, adverbs, similes, metaphors. Words. Words.

SLEDGE KICKED THE FAT MAN IN THE GROIN AND SENT HIM TUMBLING DOWN THE STAIRS LIKE A BROKEN SCREAMING DOLL, SCREAMING OUT THE WORDS OF HIS PAIN.

Agony in my head, in my leg, in my wounded forefinger. Roaring in my ears that had nothing to do with the crowd.

CULP 8566, SACKETT 7930.

Gain of ten—ten words! I wanted to laugh, locked the

sound in my throat instead, and made myself glance across at Culp. His body curved into a humpbacked C, fingers hooked into claws, expression of torment on his wet face: The strain was starting to tell on him, too. But up on the board, his prose was still pouring out in letters as bright as golden blood.

SHE WAS SO TIRED AS SHE TRUDGED ACROSS THE DUSTY SANDS OF DENEB, SO VERY TIRED. BUT SHE HAD TO GO ON, SHE HAD TO FIND THE GREEN, THE BRIGHT GREEN, THE BEAUTIFUL GREEN, IT SEEMED AS IF THERE HAD NEVER BEEN ANYTHING IN HER LIFE EXCEPT THE SEARCH AND THE ALL-CONSUMING NEED FOR THE GREEN.

I imagined again the urgent cries from Sally, from Mom and Dad: "Don't give up, Rex! There's still hope, there's still a chance!" Then they faded, and everything else seemed to fade too. I was losing all track of time and place; I felt as if I were being closed into a kind of vacuum. I couldn't hear anything, couldn't see anything but the words, always the words appearing like great and meaningless symbols on the paper and in the sky. It was just The Cranker and me now, alone together in the stadium. Winning and losing didn't even matter any more. All that mattered was the two of us and the job we were compelled to do.

Finished page out, new page in.

THE FAT MAN SAT BLEEDING AGAINST THE WALL WHERE SLEDGE'S SLUGS HAD HURLED HIM. HE WAS STILL ALIVE BUT NOT FOR LONG. "ALL RIGHT, SHAMUS," HE CROAKED, "I'M FINISHED, IT'S BIG CASINO FOR ME. BUT YOU'LL NEVER GET THE DIAMOND. I'LL TAKE IT TO HELL WITH ME FIRST."

Carriage return, tab key.

The board:

CULP 8916, SACKETT 8341.

And The Cranker's prose still coming, still running.

THE BEAST LOOMED BEFORE HER IN THE THICKET AND SHE FELT HER HEART SKIP A BEAT.

166

SHE FELT DIZZY, AS IF SHE WOULD FAINT AT ANY SECOND. I CAN'T GO THROUGH WITH THIS, SHE THOUGHT. HOW CAN I GO ON LIKE THIS? I NEED

The Cranker's machine stopped chattering then, as if he'd come to the end of a page. I was barely aware of its silence at first, but when five or six seconds had passed an awareness penetrated that it hadn't started up again. The noise from the stands seemed to have shifted cadence, to have taken on a different tenor; that penetrated too. I brought my head up and squinted across the Line.

Culp was sitting sideways in his chair, waving frantically at the sidelines. As I watched, one of his Servos came racing out with a container of Fuel. The Head Editor began waving the blue-and-yellow flag, blowing short blasts on his whistle.

Fuel penalty. The Cranker was taking a voluntary twenty-second Fuel penalty.

It was the first crack in his rigid control—but I didn't react to it one way or the other. The crack was too small and it had come too late: A twenty-second penalty at this stage of the game, with the score at 8960 to 8419, wouldn't make any difference in the outcome. It might enable me to cut the final margin to four hundred or less, but that was about all.

I didn't watch Culp take his Fuel this time; I just lowered my head and kept on punching, summoning the last reserves of my endurance.

"Culp, Culp—give us the pulp!"

As soon as the chant went up from his rooters, I knew that the penalty time was about to elapse. I raised my eyes' just long enough to check the score and to see The Cranker hunched over his typewriter, little drops of Fuel leaking down over his chin like lost words.

CULP 8960, SACKETT 8512.

His machine began to hammer again.

The illusion that I was about to collapse returned, but it wasn't the result of another block; it was just the exhaustion and the terrific mental pressure. An eight-thousand-word match was enervating enough, but ten thousand words would stretch the staying power of even the greatest of the twentieth-century prosemakers. It was why the Prose Bowl was the Prose Bowl, of course. Yet it seemed almost cruel to expect it of us, almost inhuman. . . .

My speed was holding and the words were still spewing out in a linear fashion as I headed into the final confrontation scene. They seemed jumbled to me, incoherent, except that there was no lock and no penalty flag.

SLEDGE KNEW THE UGLY TRUTH NOW AND IT WAS LIKE THE BLADE OF A SAWTOOTH KNIFE CARVING JAGGED PIECES FROM THE TENDER FLESH OF HIS PSYCHE. HE KNEW WHO HAD THE MICAWBER DIAMOND AND WHO HAD HELPED THE FAT MAN MURDER MILES CHANDLER. HE KNEW EVERYTHING NOW.

Thirty-five pages complete and thirty-six in the typewriter.

CULP 9333, SACKETT 8946.

Less than seven hundred words to go. The Prose Bowl was almost over. Just you and me, Cranker, I thought. All right, old man, let's get it done.

More words rolled out—fifty, a hundred.

And all at once there was a collective gasping sound from the crowd, the kind of sudden stunned reaction you hear in a packed stadium when something unexpected has happened. It got through to me, made me straighten up.

The Head Editor's brown-and-orange penalty flag, the one that meant Confused Narrative, was up and semaphoring. I realized then that The Cranker's machine had gone silent. My eyes sought the board and read his printout in disbelief.

"I WANT YOU," SHE SAID TO THE CREATURE, "I WANT YOU AS THE SHORES OF NEPTUNE WANT THE RESTLESS PROBING SEAS AS THE SEAS WANT THE DEPTHS GARBAGE GARBAGE

I kept staring at the board, still flailing at the keyboard, my subconscious vomiting out the words of my prose. I couldn't seem to grasp what had happened; Culp's words made no sense to me. Some of the fans were booing lustily. Over in G Section, the Sackett Boosters began chanting with renewed excitement.

"*Metaphor Kid! Make your bid!*"

The Cranker was just sitting there behind his machine with a strange, stricken look on his face. His mouth was open, his lips moving; it seemed as though he was talking to himself. Babbling to himself?

I finished page thirty-six, pulled it out blindly, and reached for another sheet of paper. Just as I brought it into the platen, Culp's machine unlocked and he hit the keys again.

But not for long.

I CAN'T WRITE THIS SHIT ANYMORE

Lock into silence. Penalty flag.

I understood then, with a kind of terrible clarity: The Cranker had broken under the pressure, the crack had become a crevasse and collapsed his professional control. I had known it to happen before, but never in the Prose Bowl. And never to a pulpeteer who was only a few hundred words from victory.

CULP 9449, SACKETT 9228.

The penalty flag came down.

GARBAGE

And the flag went back up, and the boos echoed like mad epithets in the hot afternoon.

Culp's face was contorted with emotion, wet with something more than sweat, something that could only be tears. He was weeping. The Cranker was *weeping.*

A sense of tragedy, of compassion touched me. And then it was gone, erased by another perception of the radiant numerals on the board: CULP 9449, SACKETT 9296. And erased, too, by a sudden jolt of discovery, belated from fatigue. I was only down by a hundred and fifty words now; if The Cranker didn't recover at the end of this penalty, if he took yet another one, I would be able to pull even.

I could still beat him.

I could still win the Prose Bowl.

"Do it, Rex! Grind that text!"

"IT WAS YOU ALL ALONG, VELDA," SLEDGE HAMMERED AT HER. "YOU SET MILES UP FOR THE FAT MAN. NOBODY ELSE BESIDES ME AND OLD MAN MICAWBER KNEW HE WOULD BE GUARDING THE ROCK THAT NIGHT, AND MICAWBER'S IN THE CLEAR."

Penalty flag down.

ALL GARBAGE

Penalty flag up.

Virgin paper into my typewriter. Words, sentences, paragraphs. Another half-page completed.

SHIT, The Cranker's printout said.

A rage of boos. And screams, cheers, applause, from the Boosters in G Section.

SACKETT 9481, CULP 9449.

I'd caught up, I'd taken the lead. . . .

VELDA REACHED INSIDE THE FRONT OF HER DRESS, BETWEEN HER MAGNIFICENT BREASTS. "YOU WANT THE DIAMOND?" SHE SCREAMED AT HIM. "ALL RIGHT, SAM, HERE IT IS!" SHE HURLED THE GLITTERING STONE AT HIM, THEN DOVE SIDEWAYS TO HER PURSE AND YANKED OUT A SMALL PEARL-HANDLED AUTOMATIC. BUT SHE NEVER HAD THE CHANCE TO USE IT. HATING HER, HATING HIMSELF, HATING THIS ROTTEN PAINFUL BUSINESS HE WAS IN, SLEDGE FIRED TWICE FROM THE HIP.

"Hack it, Sackett, hack it, Sackett, hack it, Sackett!"

More words.

Clean page.

More words.

SACKETT 9702, CULP 9449.

And The Cranker was on his feet, stumbling away from his machine, stumbling around in circles on the lonely field, his hands clasped to his face, tears leaking through his shaky old fingers.

TEARS LEAKED FROM SLEDGE'S EYES AS HE LOOKED DOWN AT WHAT WAS LEFT OF THE BEAUTIFUL AND TREACHEROUS VELDA LYING CRUMPLED ON THE CARPET. ALL HE WANTED TO DO NOW WAS TO GET OUT OF THERE, GO HOME TO SALLY, NO, SALLY HAD LEFT HIM A LONG TIME AGO AND THERE WAS NOBODY WAITING AT HOME ANYMORE, NOBODY AT ALL. HE WAS SO TIRED HE COULDN'T THINK STRAIGHT.

Two of Culp's Servos had come out on the grass and were steadying him, supporting him between them. Leading him away.

New page, old words. A few more words.

SLEDGE SENT HIS CAR SLIDING QUICKLY THROUGH THE COLD WET RAIN, ALONG THE MEAN STREETS OF THE JUNGLE THAT WAS THE CITY. IT WAS ALMOST OVER NOW. HE NEEDED A LONG REST AND HE DIDN'T KNOW IF HE COULD GO ON BEING A PRIVATE RICHARD EVEN AFTER HE'D HAD IT, BUT RIGHT NOW HE JUST DIDN'T CARE.

Pandemonium in the stands.

Word count at 9985.

AND SAM SLEDGE, AS LONELY AND EMPTY AS THE NIGHT ITSELF, DROVE FASTER TOWARD HOME.

THE END.

The claxon sounded.

Above the din the amplified voice of the P.A. announcer began shouting, "Final score: Rex Sackett 10,000, Leon Culp 9449. Rex Sackett, The Metaphor Kid, is the new Prose Bowl champion!"

Fans were spilling out of the stands; security Servos came rushing out to throw a protective cordon around me. The rest of the crowd stamped their feet and shrieked my name at the top of their lungs—the loudest, most reverberating sound I'd ever heard.

But I didn't move; I didn't do anything at all. I just sat there, letting it all wash over me and around me, and stared up at the board.

I had won.

And I didn't feel anything at all.

PART FOUR

Truth and Consequences

1

The Cranker was waiting for me in my locker room.

I still wasn't feeling anything when my Servos and those from the security detail delivered me to the door, ten minutes after the final horn. I didn't want to see anybody while I had that emptiness. Not the New-Sport scribes and TriDim announcers. Not even Sally or Mom and Dad.

I told the League official who came up and the security Servos that I wanted to be alone, no visitors of any kind, for at least fifteen minutes. Then I went into the locker room and hurried over to the container of Fuel. I had three ounces poured out and in my hand when Culp came out of the alcove where the Body-Ease was.

"Hello, kid," he said.

I stared at him. His sudden appearance had taken me by surprise and I couldn't think of anything to say.

"I came over under the stands after they took me off," he said. "One of the security Servos is a friend of mine and he let me in. You mind?"

A little shakily, I took some of the Fuel. It helped me find my voice. "No," I said, "I don't mind, Cranker."

"Leon," he said. "Just plain Leon Culp. The Cranker is dead; to hell with The Cranker."

"That's not so. The Cranker is still alive; you're still the best there is, no matter what happened today. A legend . . ."

He laughed—a hoarse, humorless sound. He'd had a lot

more Fuel before coming over here, I could see that. Still, he looked better than he had on the field, more composed. I might even have thought he was The Cranker of old if it hadn't been for the look in his eyes. It was the same look that had been in Ollie Garbowitz's eyes after our semifinal match last week—that mixture of personal tragedy, bitterness, emptiness, sorrow, and pain.

Culp said, "Legend?" There aren't any legends, kid. Just pros, good and bad—all of us the same except for shades of more or less talent. And the best of us are remembered only as long as we keep on winning, stay near the top. Nobody gives a damn about the has-beens and the losers."

"The fans could never forget you—"

"The fans? Hell, you heard them out there when the pressure got to me and I lost it in the stretch. Boos, nothing but boos: no compassion at all. It's just a game to them. You think they understand what it's like for us inside, the loneliness, the overload of feeling? You think they understand it's not a game for us at all?" He shook his shaggy old head. "No, kid, the fans would finish me if I hadn't already finished myself. They know I'm washed up; they know it's all over."

"You're not washed up, Cranker—"

"I told you, don't call me Cranker any more. It's a goddamn silly nickname that the media pasted on me, just like they paste them on all of us. But we don't have to use them among ourselves. We've got real names, haven't we?"

I remembered Ollie Garbowitz saying the same thing last Sunday; I hadn't given it much thought, but now that Culp pointed it out again it did seem that he and Ollie were right. We *didn't* have to call ourselves by what the media called us.

"All right . . . Leon," I said. "But you're not washed up. You'll come back next season."

"The hell I will," Culp said. "This was my last shot; I know that and so does everybody else. If I even suited up next year I'd be lucky to finish the season in last place in the Mainstream Commercial Fic League, playing before a lot of empty seats and plenty of boos from the ones that were filled."

"But what'll you do?"

"Who knows?" he said. "I never saved any of the money; I'm almost as broke now as when I started out thirty-five years ago. Maybe I can get an Assistant Editor's job, or a private coaching assignment in the Junior Creative League. Otherwise I guess I'll become a Servo—anything to buy eats and Fuel."

"A Servo? You can't become a Servo."

"Why can't I?"

"Because . . . well, because you're too good for that kind of menial job; you're an important person, one of the great pulpeteers. . . ."

He looked at me hard for about ten seconds, so hard that it made me uneasy. Then he said, "You really are a slow learner, aren't you, kid? You just don't want to understand anything."

I frowned at him. "What do you mean by that?"

"You think we're important, huh?"

"Of course I do."

"Well, we're not. Seventy-five years ago the people in Old-Sport—baseball and football players, the lot of them—thought they were important too. But who remembers them today? Who remembers Old-Sport at all? And even more to the point, who remembers the prosemakers of two hundred or one hundred or even sixty years ago? Nobody except pulpeteers like us, who make our living copying them, feeding off their work like parasites."

"Parasites?"

"That's right. There isn't a one of us who's had an original thought since New-Sport began."

"Then . . . then you meant what you typed out there at the end? About our prose being garbage?"

"You bet your young ass I meant it," Culp said. "And that's one of the reasons, along with corruption and the general shape of the society, why New-Sport won't last anywhere near as long as Old-Sport did; fifty or a hundred years from now we'll be as obsolete and forgotten as Babe Ruth, Joe

Namath, and the rest of them. Or as obsolete and forgotten as Jack Woodford and any other prosemaker you'd care to name."

He was confusing me. "What are you saying?" I asked him. "Are you saying we're no better than Servos?"

"Jesus Christ!" Culp said in an exasperated voice. He reached for my Fuel container and had a long swallow from it without even asking permission. "No better than Servos?" he said then. "We *are* Servos, kid, *that's* what I'm saying. And useless Servos at that because we don't even perform a worthwhile public service."

"That's not true—"

"It's true, all right. Give it some thought; maybe you'll see just how true it is before it's too late."

"Too late?"

"Too late," Culp said earnestly. "Here's a little advice: Make the Prose Bowl your last competition. Retire, marry your girl, get the hell out of New-Sport. You've got the prize money; invest it right and you can live on it for the rest of your life, you'll never have to write another line. Go out a winner, kid, because if you don't maybe someday you'll go out just like me."

He raised a hand in a kind of awkward salute and shuffled over to the door.

"Leon—wait."

He turned.

"What you said to me the other night in the Ultradome, about not worrying because I'd get Sally back all right. You said that part was fixed too, like all of pulpeteering. What did you mean?"

Culp didn't say anything for a time; then he shrugged. "There's a Futuristic Fic story from the 1940s called 'Typewriter in the Sky,' " he said, "by a prosemaker named L. Ron Hubbard. The main character gets plucked out of the world he lives in and thrust into another world, a make-believe world, and all because a wordsmith he knows is writing a story about that make-believe place; he's trapped there, manipulated by the wordsmith's imagination. At the end the protagonist is returned to his own world and has a sudden insight; he looks up at the sky and thinks: Up there—God? In a dirty bathrobe?"

I just looked at him. "That's ridiculous," I said. "You can't believe a weird idea like that could actually be true—that there's some prosemaker . . . up there . . . writing all of *us.*"

A small bitter smile curved his mouth. "Well, you know how it is, kid," he said. "A crazy old hack like me is liable to believe anything." And he turned again and went out into the tunnel. The door slid shut behind him; he was gone.

I sat down in front of the Fuel container, poured out another three ounces, drank them down. The emptiness was gone now; I could feel again, waves of feeling that broke and swirled through me. But it was all confusion, all ambivalence again: New-Sport was good, New-Sport was bad; I wanted to be a pulpeteer, I didn't want to be a pulpeteer; I understood everything, I understood nothing.

If New-Sport was good, as I'd always believed, then the corruption last year and this year were just isolated incidents and might never happen again. And it was just exhaustion and the terrible pressure of the past week that had left me feeling so hollow at the end of the Face-Off. The joy would come later, with the interviews and the endorsements and the celebrity TriDim appearances. And the money would come too, more money than I'd ever dreamed of in my life—not just this year but next year and the year after that and all the years to come.

If New-Sport was bad, then I'd felt so hollow because the insight I'd had at halftime was the right one: Culp and I were soul brothers and in going up against him I was going up against myself; all pulpeteers were the same, so beating him would be, and *was,* a little like beating myself. And even though it had been Culp who had broken under the pressure, it could just as easily have been Rex Sackett—could still be Rex Sackett in some other match, some other Prose Bowl, typing GARBAGE GARBAGE and then stumbling around on a lonely field, weeping.

Go out a winner, kid, because if you don't maybe someday you'll go out just like me.

Maybe he was right; maybe he and Sally were both right.

But maybe they weren't and what had happened to Culp would never happen to me.

And I just couldn't help thinking, over in one corner of my mind, that there had never been a successful championship defense or a two-time Prose Bowl winner. . . .

> Mud, mud, glorious mud,
> Nothing quite like it for cooling the blood;
> So follow me, follow—
> Down to the hollow—
> And there we shall wallow in mud
> Glo-o-o-o-ri-ous mud!